Celtic Legends
The Search for the White Bear Talisman

R. B. Butler

Grosvenor House
Publishing Limited

This book is published by
Grosvenor House Publishing Ltd
Link House
140 The Broadway, Tolworth, Surrey, KT6 7HT.
www.grosvenorhousepublishing.co.uk

A CIP record for this book
is available from the British Library

Paperback ISBN 978-1-80381-041-6
Hardback ISBN 978-1-80381-040-9

Written for and dedicated to my daughters.
Took longer than expected.

Chapter 1

The Druid Council

The renowned prophet, Shylah, had summoned all the druid leaders to the great meeting place that they called *Ynys Môn*. This was a holy place with deep mystical and magical powers that was fiercely guarded by the most loyal and trusted Celtic soldiers. Shylah was the great Lyn y Fan (Lady of the Lake). She had the gift of vision and could see all things that had been and some things yet to pass. She was a half druid, half Goddess spirit who was eternally bound to the water and she possessed the power to appear in any body of water whether it be a lake, river or pool, but she could never tread on dry land as she was trapped within her realm by a curse that was placed upon her many years ago. Her beauty was legendary. She had long black hair that shimmered gracefully down to her waist, as smooth as silk without a single wave or curl. She had bright blue-green eyes that looked like clear waters on a hot summer's day and a complexion that matched the sandy beaches on the coast. She wore a long, shimmering, silver dress that shone like glass and reflected the rippling waters beneath her feet. As she stood on the surface held aloft by a magical force Shylah eyed the crowd that had gathered to see her.

On the bank were many important druid leaders including Tiernon the mighty, who was the brother to Shylah. He was the most powerful druid that ever lived because he held in his palms the power to produce bolts of lightning. A power that was given to him as a gift from his father Taranis, the God of Thunder. When he received this power at his coming of age the shock was so great that it turned two strands of his dark hair and beard grey, making him look much older and worldlier than his younger sister.

He was slender; dressed in a long white robe tied at the waist with a large hood that he seldom wore on his head, which flowed majestically between his shoulders. Attached to his belt was a scabbard that concealed within it a long Celtic sword.

Among the gathering other druids were similarly dressed but they lacked the majesty of Tiernon. There was an aura of power about his presence.

The large crowd was facing Shylah, anxiously waiting for her to speak. When she did speak it was softly yet with authority, "I have called you to council today for I have something of great importance to tell you. I have foreseen the birth of a king in a land far away to the east. He will be wise and truthful, but he shall perish at the hands of his own people for his beliefs. He shall change the hearts of men and a powerful race will bring forth a new faith to our shores. They will conquer many of our lands and settle in our country decimating our kind, calling us pagans. They will turn our religion to theirs our language to theirs and our culture and the old ways will be lost."

A murmur sounded around the crowd as they gave uneasy glances towards each other as Shylah continued her prophecy.

"Many years from this day, after twelve generations have passed by, our soldiers will fight bravely against the organised armies of the new faith bringers, but I warn you now that they will fail."

The crowd shuffled uneasily as Shylah continued.

"There is a small glimmer of hope. We are to carefully watch the Clans of the Brigantes. The most powerful will meet in battle and the victorious king will die on that day and leave a wife with his unborn offspring. From her bosom will sprout twins. These are the chosen ones who will embark upon a quest that will not be without peril. The Evil One will endeavour to thwart the twins in

2

their quest. It is up to you Tiernon, and you alone, to show your presence upon the battlefield to protect the Queen from that day forward. You will become the protector of the twins and you will make them ready for their task."

Tiernon gave a stern glance as he asked, "What is this task?"

Shylah paused a moment before continuing with her prophecy.

"At their coming of age the chosen ones are to journey south in search of Elgon, the swamp dragon, and retrieve a sacred stone that was lost many years ago. They must protect this stone, keeping it from the reach of evil and return it to Hogarth the red dragon of the western mountains. In return for this favour the red dragon will reveal your destiny and send you on a quest in search of the white bear talisman, but the detail of this quest remains hidden from my vision. Take heed of these words for the swamp dragon is no easy foe. He has crushed the people in that realm and holds them prisoner within the dark caves, for they keep the stone from his grasp which he tightens, year on year, in the hope that they will succumb to his wishes and relinquish the sacred stone. Failure to retrieve this gem from the clutches of the Evil One will result in the death and destruction of our people and culture in the generations to come."

Tiernon stared sternly towards the sky as if talking to his Maker. He held his arms aloft and said, "With the power given to me by my father, I will protect the chosen ones and make certain that this journey does not fail, or die trying. Woe betide any evil that stands in my way for I hold within my palms the wrath of my father."

Tiernon summoned a great power from within and sent into the sky two great bolts of lightning that lit up the whole crowd as they yelled in surprise and fear.

*

The council continued into the night. Important matters were discussed and quests were given to other druid leaders, but these are for other stories.

Chapter 2

The Battle for Brigantes

Two years had passed since the druid council. The early morning sun was shining and there was a cool breeze in the air bringing with it a mist from over the horizon.

From within a high spot in the great tower of the fort the lookout could see far across the valley for many miles. He could see the vast fields that his ancestors had cleared for their animals and buildings. There were cattle, brown sheep and goats all grazing peacefully together. To his left were fields of flax, wheat and oats swaying in the breeze and to his right was a large field of willow.

Scattered amongst the fields and animals on the lower hills were several smaller forts, each with their own protective perimeters and an array of huts that were adorned with thatched roofs and white walls. He could see into their gardens where the pigs and grouse were busy nosing around, trying their best to reach the vegetables and herb patches which were fenced with willow for protection.

A group of soldiers had gathered outside the smaller forts and had begun scrambling swiftly up the hillside. To the east he could see the marshes. These were vast, green valleys of untouched landscape and were reminiscent of the way the land was before man had drained it to make way for buildings and crops. It was not wise to venture too deep into the marshes. Fairy folk, bog beasts and other creatures lived there. The river from the north ran down beside the marsh as far as his eyes could see.

In the distance was the great forest that stretched out for many miles. The forest was a dangerous, dark, dense place and not for the faint hearted.

As he panned the landscape looking as far as his eyes would allow, he finally spotted a large procession of clansmen on their way northwards from the south, roughly twenty miles away. They were marching towards the fort to meet his clansmen in the field nearby. Their intention was to take ownership of the land by force. The oncoming clan was of no surprise to the lookout, he knew that they would come. The peace talks from the week before had been unsuccessful. The battle was set, and the meeting place arranged.

The lookout knew that he must warn his tribe that the southern Brigantes were upon them and without wasting a single second, he drew a large horn from his belt and blew it as loud as his lungs would allow. Everyone heard it and at that very moment everyone stopped what they were doing. A farmer who was ploughing one of the many fields just outside the fort, reined in the large bullock that was doing most of the work to a standstill and ran towards the fort. Two soldiers who were mastering their techniques of unarmed combat ran to their military quarters to take up amour and weapons. King Cedric of the north was in council with his advisors. When he heard the great horn he slammed his fist on the table and rushed outside to rally his army.

The nobles and King Cedric assembled just outside the fort. The lookout opened the gates in readiness for them.

*

The clans from the lower hills had now gathered outside to meet the king. It was a frightening sight to see. Some soldiers had gathered on their chariots, powered by large ponies that were strong in stature and well suited for pulling the vehicles at speed. The soldiers were fully dressed for battle in brightly coloured woollen, red tartan trousers that had been dyed with the root of the madder plant, blue tartan robes that got their colour from the leaves of the woad plant and plain, bright red shirts that were dyed with blackcurrant juices. They had huge spears in their right hands, axes on their belts and swords on the left side in long scabbards. Foot soldiers flanked the left side wielding large spears and short swords, but they carried huge shields that were brightly painted and decorated with various animal images. They had taken the time to paint woad on their faces, which made them look even more menacing. King Cedric and his nobles were astride their regal ponies. The king's dress was the most impressive, adorned in jewellery which included a thick, gold necklace, armband and a gold brooch which held his robe together at the collar. He wore bronze wrist protectors as well as bronze shin guards, all highly decorated with great skill. His helmet had a great carving on the nose guard of a stag's head with antlers sprouting on either side to form the eyebrows. Only the nobility wore headgear to show off their status in battle.

*

King Cedric rode forward to the front of the procession and spoke to his soldiers. "The day has arrived when we meet in battle the southern clans. If we die this day, may it be with honour and may the living honour the brave."

He then took his sword from its scabbard and waved it in the air whilst skilfully handling his pony as it reared on its hind legs, as he shouted. "Those who are with me say so now."

Hearing his words, the whole procession of what must have been over a thousand strong, waved their weapons in the air and screamed a blood-curdling scream that would frighten even the bravest of warriors. Just as the noise died down the lookout blew his horn three times and the procession began to march towards their oppressors.

*

Both southern and northern Brigantes clans marched towards each other for a good while until coming to a standstill roughly three hundred yards apart. Both sides were mirror images of each other, using almost identical battle formations and wearing similar clothes and weapons. The only differing features were the blue patterns painted on their faces that distinguished one clan from the other. Their chosen fighting ground was a large field, about four miles from the fort, where the land flattened out.

The nobles and kings sat patiently behind the battle line and King Cedric beckoned his General to dismount and meet the enemies General in the open space betwixt the two rivals. They uttered a few words together, unheard by the others and then headed back towards the battle line. Upon reaching the line of the northern clan, the General spoke loudly to King Cedric, "There will be no pardon today. The battle will commence."

As quickly as the last word had fallen from his mouth the whole clan of the north erupted in cheer. The foot soldiers on either side of the battle line quickly stuck their spears into the ground. They took their shields from their backs and drew their swords, using the hilts to drum their shields. The sound was deafening yet melodic and tuneful. It was like the hooves of a thousand ponies galloping across the land. Simultaneously, both camps chanted in unison. Each clan gave the other side the chance to respond as if a competition was underway for who could make the loudest and most menacing song. Suddenly there was a deadly silence, which lasted for about a second, but felt like an age. Then, as if prompted by an unseen signal, the chariot riders on both sides whipped their ponies into action, racing chariot towards chariot at blinding speed. Chariot riders crashed into each other with pony, rider and chariot hurtling forward by the force. Other riders tipped over bumps in the ground in mid-flight.

Those that passed each other drove out their spears in a stabbing motion and some threw them at one another with deadly accuracy, hitting the enemy cleanly. Others missed and their spears were lost to the ground. This part of the battle was short lived. It was not long before both sides were on foot and without chariots. At this point their short swords were drawn and they fought each other fiercely in the centre, stabbing brutally at the necks in a downward motion between the clavicles. Some fighters opted for a stab to the ribs and some warriors simply slashed at the neck, taking heads off with one swipe. Some drew out their axes, carving at the enemy wildly. One person was hit clean in the jaw, almost cutting through the entire bottom half of his face. Surprisingly, he fought on until a large woman cleaved him at the back of the neck with her sword, breaking the bone. The foot soldiers had put their swords back into their scabbards and with shield in one hand for protection and long spears in the other they charged into battle.

*

This was the most blood curdling part of the whole battle. The foot soldiers used their long spears to skewer the injured and helpless. Some were killed outright, some were badly mauled around the legs, arms, or abdomen and some were hit so hard that the spears snapped as they went through bone. However, death followed quickly and it was not long before the soldiers had used up all their spears. They all drew their swords successfully skewering the enemy giving swift end, with stabs to the neck, lungs or face. Once the foot soldiers were in full battle it was time for the nobles of both sides to join the fray, including the two kings. This was the most honourable part of the battle. The nobles rushed into the battle on their large ponies, clashing together brutally with swords drawn. King Cedric was very brutal, swishing off the heads and arms of anyone that came close. It was a good half an hour of slashing, cutting and stabbing one another before there emerged a clear victory.

The northern clan won out, eventually killing or maiming nearly every single member of the southern clan. Each member of the stronger northern Brigantes began systematically hacking off the heads of the enemy and tying them by the hair to their belts so that the heads hung by their legs. The battle was almost over as King Cedric dismounted from his ride and approached the enemy king. He grasped him by his shoulder and spun him round so that he could see his face. With sword in the air he was about to offer the final blow, but as quickly as the southern king was spun around he produced a small dagger from an unseen place and stuck it in the throat of King Cedric. In response, King Cedric quickly decapitated his enemy, but it was clear by the shock on his face that his wound was severe.

He clutched his throat and gasped for air as blood pumped through his fingers. The battle was over; the northern clan systematically slaughtered their enemies one by one. Meanwhile some of the foot soldiers gathered an upturned chariot and regained a pony. The soldiers lifted King Cedric into the chariot and took him back to the fort. They packed his wound with sphagnum moss to staunch the bleeding, but the king's breathing was staggered. The king was without voice, for the wound had cut his throat so deep that blood was still coming from the wound, albeit slowly. His life force was leaving him. He had turned drip white as he died, barely a hundred yards from the fort gates. All the men and women fell to their knees, wailing in horror. A crowd rushed through the opened gates to join the mourners. Queen Pictania fought her way to the king and knelt beside him. She could not speak but sobbed uncontrollably. Suddenly, a voice of authority called out.

"Do not weep, for this day is a good day. The king has not died in vain; what he has done this day was foretold. His children will deliver our people."

The queen looked up through tear filled eyes and saw Tiernon the mighty in front of her. He had appeared as if from nowhere. Queen Pictania was vexed and responded angrily, "Where were you when our people most needed you? You were supposed to protect us."

She was so angry that she stood up and thought of striking Tiernon with her fists, but even through grief she thought it best not to; Tiernon was very powerful and could strike her down with thunder.

Tiernon grabbed her by the shoulders and embraced her. With tears in his eyes he spoke softly in her ear, "I am truly sorry that I was not in a position to save your king, for it was forbidden by the Gods. It has been foretold that the victor of this great battle would die, leaving his beloved wife with children."

The queen looked at him both surprised and still tearful. "I am not with child."

Tiernon looked at the queen knowingly as he replied, "Your husband has left you with the beginning of tiny life inside your womb. If I am correct you will bear two children and these will be the chosen ones. However, there is only one way to tell. You must seek out Brigitte, the Goddess of Fertility. She will acknowledge that my judgement is correct and from that day forward they will grow within you. The twins will have the spirit and courage of your husband and they will save our people."

The queen was struggling to take in this new information and inquired, "What will they save our people from?"

Tiernon placed his hand reassuringly on the Queen's shoulders as he replied, "They will save us from eternal destruction. What your husband has done this day has paved the way for our kind. The Gods will honour him and will send him back to earth as one of God's creatures. Mark my words, his life was not wasted."

The queen seemed eased by these words. They went inside the fort to her private quarters and Tiernon spoke more to the queen, repeating most of what had been told to him at the druid's council by Shylah. Armed with the full facts the queen seemed less grieved than before. She summoned her council and told them to prepare her in readiness for her new role as the clan leader.

*

Over the next few days whilst preparations were underway, the northern Brigantes clan gathered the bodies of the dead, including the enemies and both kings. They dug a large hole and placed the bodies one by one into the huge void. The clan showed respect to their enemies. All the clansmen and women gathered around, singing and chanting prayers, asking the Gods to accept the dead. Tiernon said a few words in honour of the King.

*

Many days passed and the Queen was now ready to take power over northern Brigantes. All the clansmen and women gathered around the edge of the huge marsh next to the fort. They were casting gold cups and thick gold necklaces into the swamps whilst chanting and singing.

Queen Pictania walked slowly towards the marsh with a procession of followers who were playing instruments of music, including flutes and small harps. Tiernon was at her side. The crowd parted and bowed as she passed. Upon reaching the edge of the marsh Queen Pictania produced a large goblet from within one of her long sleeves as she spoke softly, "I offer my troth to the Gods that I will serve my people well and with honesty and fairness. May the Gods protect my people from famine and war from this day till the end of my reign."

She then hurled the goblet into the swamps and as it sank the crowd said in unison, "The Gods have accepted your pledge."

Cheering and singing followed and the whole crowd began to party with music, dancing and plenty of beer drinking. The party went on into the night; this was a celebration to mark the Gods' acceptance of a new ruler.

During the festivities Tiernon caught a chance to speak to the Queen. He told her of his own pledge to protect her until the birth of the twins and assured her that she could trust him implicitly.

*

The days were drawing closer to Beltane and Queen Pictania was growing more and more anxious for the arrival of the Goddess Brigit. She found herself wondering what it would be like to feel new life growing within her.

Chapter 3

The Changeling

It was the morning of Beltane on the first day in May. Celebrations were in full swing. Everyone was merrymaking dancing and lighting bonfires. This was a way of expressing love and thanks to the Gods for new life and prosperity.

The celebrations went on well into the night.

As the moon reached its highest point Tiernon approached the Queen. "It is time to make ready for your acceptance for Brigit to acknowledge your unborn as the chosen ones."

The Queen was nervous. She had looked forward to this day for so long but now it was upon her she was afraid and unsure, so she confided in Tiernon. "What am I to do? How will I recognise the Goddess Brigit?"

Tiernon held her by the hand as he spoke reassuringly to her, "You must enter the forest that lies just outside the fort, unaided by any mortal being."

He paused for a moment and then continued, "You must venture through the forest until you come to the first clearing. You will know the way. There you must lie on the ground with your eyes closed and no matter what you hear, you must not open them until Brigit has inspected you. Do not fear as you have the Gods for protection."

Queen Pictania was afraid yet also excited.

Tiernon led the Queen to the forest. He then left her side and she continued her journey alone. Taking a deep breath she entered the depths of the great forest. She was terrified. Somehow she knew the direction she must take and without much thought she proceeded into the dark thickets and tall trees that enveloped her. She could see the tiny eyes of the forest gazing out at her; some were natural creatures, others were small fairy folk. Trembling with every step she reached the great clearing that Tiernon had spoken about. She walked to the centre and lay on the ground with her eyes tight shut.

Tiernon spoke to her with the power of his mind. "No matter what you fear do not open your eyes, for you are safe."

The Queen lay still for what seemed an eternity until she heard a rustling amongst the foliage. A great beast of the forest was drawing ever near. She could hear its breath as it sniffed the forest floor as if trailing her scent. It drew closer and closer and was then upon her, sniffing at her face. She could feel its cold wet nose on her neck and smell its musky breath. She almost opened her eyes but knew this would not be a wise thing to do. The beast was a deer. It sniffed at her and nuzzled her belly. The Queen suddenly felt very strange, then the beast spoke softly to her.

"You are the chalice that carries the new life of the chosen ones. From your bosom will sprout great warriors and guardians of your culture. Put your faith in Tiernon for his task is to protect your children. You have my blessing gracious queen. You are the one."

Silence fell upon the forest and the deer was gone. Queen Pictania was about to open her eyes when she heard the rustling and snarling of what sounded like a large ferocious beast. She was now totally petrified and covered her face with both hands to keep herself from opening her eyes. The beast was a very large black wolf. It approached stealthily and purposefully towards her, baring its teeth and growling. It sniffed at her face and body until it reached her belly. The beast took particular interest in that area. The possibility crossed the Queen's thoughts that the beast was about to eat her when suddenly the great wolf snarled and was gone.

Queen Pictania was so overwhelmed with fear that she rose and ran out of the forest blindly, with branches lashing at her face causing small cuts, until finally she found the arms of Tiernon as he reached out for her with reassurance.

"Calm down my Queen, your task is over. The beast you heard was Delano, the pooka. He has been sent by the Gods to protect your children. He was collecting their unborn scent so that he will know them when they meet again in the future."

He then led her safely back to the fort and she retired to her quarters to bed. Exhausted she fell straight to sleep and into a dream state. She dreamt about her twins a boy and a girl, and saw them at the age of about three. They were playing together in their bed quarters, giggling, and all was happy until she noticed a grizzly figure in the doorway. A small creature emerged that took an almost human form, yet had an evil twisted face with many teeth in its mouth. It had long ears, arms and legs. Its fingers and toes were also elongated and its flesh was an amphibious green. The creature crept towards the children and swept them up in each arm, giving a menacing cackle as it disappeared into the darkness of the night. The Queen awoke, sweat dripping from her brow. She screamed, "Do not take my children, do not take my babies."

*

The next day she confided her dream to Tiernon. He looked concerned and told her that it would be wise to consult with his sister Shylah. They set off towards the great river that ran from the north until they arrived at the water's edge, where Tiernon began chanting. After a moment Shylah rose up from the depths of the clear water as she spoke to both Tiernon and the Queen.

"You have called to me dear brother, I know what troubles you. I have had the same vision as you, my Queen. I too have seen the changeling. He will be sent by the Evil One on the night of the twins' third birthday. If he succeeds in stealing the twins they will be lost forever."

Queen Pictania fell to her knees and responded woefully, "Spare my children. They are not yet born and evil is upon them."

Shylah gave a comforting smile towards the Queen as she replied, "From this day till that you must raise your children with loving kindness and forget what you have seen, for I will warn you when the time is right and prepare you for what must be done."

Shylah knew that words alone would not comfort the Queen, so she cast a spell upon her which erased all trace of the dream from her memory.

The Queen looked bewildered as she spoke to Tiernon, "I will go back to my quarters now."

The Queen headed back towards the fort as if led by some magical force. Tiernon waited until she was out of sight and then spoke to Shylah. "What can we do to prevent this thing from happening?"

Shylah was troubled by this question and frowned as she explained, "Nothing, but the sacrifice of one who is pure of heart with a life given willingly can stop the changeling from taking the children. You must not trouble your thoughts about this. Farewell my brother."

With these last words she sank beneath the water. Tiernon shouted loudly, "Shylah, do not go! Wait!"

Nevertheless, she was gone.

*

As Shylah had promised all was well from that day. The twins were born in February, the morning of Imbolc. This was the day associated with Brigit the Goddess of fertility. This was the season when the ewes produced milk, when the frogs spawned and when the early birds were nesting.

The birth had been difficult, lasting most of the previous night. The first twin, a boy, appeared at the first ray of sunlight, followed shortly by a girl. As usual Tiernon was quick to arrive at the side of the Queen, who lay in bed. She was weary from her ordeal.

Tiernon spoke gently, "May I see them my Queen?"

She gave him a tearful smile as she responded, "They are here, by my side."

She pulled down the cosy warm bed covers, made by her own hands from the finest hare pelts, that glistened by the firelight to reveal one tiny face on either side of her. Both babies were sleeping peacefully.

Tiernon had tears in his eyes as he spoke, "This is a truly magnificent day. They are truly beautiful my Queen."

He then bowed to his knees and held the hand of the Queen as he spoke again.

"Never before in all my long life have I witnessed anything as blessed as this moment. You have my troth that I will protect your children with my life."

The Queen looked reassured. She placed her free hand on Tiernon's head as she said, "I know you will my friend."

They had become very close over the past year. Tiernon respected her kindness and generosity towards her people and Queen Pictania respected Tiernon's integrity. He stood wiping his eyes as he said, "Oh dear, I have something in my eye."

He tried to remove an imaginary object from his eye and the Queen laughed. Tiernon gave a wry smile and said joyously, "I must tell the village. This is a day of celebration." He ran out into the open air of the fort chuckling loudly, "The twins are born! The twins are born!"

This was very odd behaviour for Tiernon the mighty. He was normally a stern man and very serious. The lookout heard him and cried, "Hooray!"

He pulled out his great horn from his belt and blew it loudly many times. The whole village had been waiting for his signal and many people began emerging from their dwellings and gathering in the open field. One man was half-dressed, still tucking his shirt into his trousers, whilst hopping about on one leg trying to put a boot on the other foot.

Lower down the hillside in the smaller forts, people were blowing horns whilst scrambling up the hillside in a large procession towards the great fort. On this day, from morning until night, was the biggest celebration since celebrations first began. Everyone was merrymaking dancing and singing. The only people in bed were the Queen and her new-born twins. They were resting in their quarters. Night was upon the fort and everyone was either tipsy or drunk; even Tiernon had drunk a goblet or two.

Suddenly a mystical force threw open the fort gates. The music stopped and the singing halted as everybody stared out into the blackness, struck dumb by the shock. Nobody moved. Nobody uttered a sound. They just stared at the open gate into the night. A wind whistled through the open gate and a large, black, four-footed creature appeared out of the shadows. It was a huge snarling wolf. Never had any man seen a wolf of such magnitude. It stood still for a moment, sniffing the air as if searching for some sort of scent trail. It had a thick mane on its neck and bright blue eyes. At last, someone found the strength to speak and shouted, "Kill the wolf! Protect the Queen!"

He was a burly fellow. He drew his sword quickly and ran towards the wolf with sword held aloft. At that moment Tiernon held his hands in the air and screamed, "Do not slay the wolf! Do not slay the wolf! This is my friend and protector of the chosen ones, sent by the Gods themselves."

The man with the sword skidded to a halt and slipped on his bottom, sliding right under the wolf's feet. Although he was a burly fellow the huge wolf dwarfed him. He was lying on his back as the wolf looked down at him, when suddenly it licked his face playfully. He thought he was about to be eaten and was calling for help. The crowd erupted in laughter for this was an amusing sight to see.

The wolf approached Tiernon and rubbed its head on the back of his hand. Tiernon looked towards the crowd as he informed them, "This is my friend, Delano. He is a Pooka. He can take the shape of a wolf, a bear, a horse and an eagle. He has shared many adventures with me in the past and is the only creature on this earth that I trust with my life."

Tiernon patted the wolf on the head and ruffled its fur as he said, "Show them your true form my friend."

The wolf began shaking with its eyes tight shut. Within a couple of seconds it changed shape into a human like figure. It unravelled in stature until standing upright, almost seven feet tall. Jet-black fur covered the beast from head to toe. The only feature that remained unchanged was its bright blue eyes. It had many sharp teeth in its mouth and long hands and feet. Even though it was large and menacing in stature, it looked like a friendly sort. It could also speak in human tongue and it said, "I am Delano, the Pooka, protector of the chosen ones. I have only one master and that is my old friend Tiernon. Any friend of his is a friend of mine."

The man whom the wolf had licked was now on his feet. He looked a little more at ease and asked the Pooka, "Do you like a drink friend?"

Delano replied with a wry smile, "I thought you would never ask."

The lookout closed the gates and the party continued as before. Tiernon found the chance to speak to Delano alone. "Tomorrow I will introduce you to the twins and my Queen. You gave her such a fright the last time you met."

Delano embraced his friend as he said, "I look forward to it."

Tiernon returned to his usual stern self and faced Delano in earnest, "This will be the hardest task we have ever undertaken. We have the Evil One against us and must stay on our guard."

The Pooka grinned, "Never fear old friend, I am always ready. I can smell trouble a mile away."

Tiernon gave a stern look as he replied. "That is why I was so pleased when the Gods chose you for this task, for I will need all the help I can get."

Delano shook his head from side to side as he said, "You worry too much; our quest is a long way off. The twins are newborn. Let us enjoy the time we have together until the twins come of age. Let us worry about the Evil One when we start our journey. That is when evil will strike and not before."

Tiernon gave a worrying glance as he replied, "I hope you are right. You are a wise one Delano."

Tiernon then proceeded to show Delano to his quarters and they retired for the night.

Chapter 4

The Sacrifice of a Pure Heart

The next day Tiernon approached the Queen. "Are you well my Queen? I hope the noise last night did not keep you awake."

She smiled softly, "After what I have been through, I would not have awoken through a thunderstorm."

Tiernon gave the Queen a smile as he said, "Remember the night in the forest when you were scared out of your wits by a huge beast?"

The Queen responded shakily, "Oh yes. You told me not to worry because the Gods had sent the beast to protect me."

Tiernon was still smiling. "Allow me to introduce him. This is the Pooka. His name is Delano. He will help me to protect you and your children."

Delano entered the room in his true form. He was so huge that he had to stoop under the doorway. The Queen, taken aback, could not quite believe the sheer size of him as she inspected him through a sideward glance, not daring to look him in the eyes.

Delano spoke reassuringly. "I am sorry for scaring you at our last meeting my lady. May I see the babies that I am bound to protect?"

The Queen was visibly shaking. She glanced in the direction of Tiernon, who reassured her. "It is alright my Queen, you are quite safe."

Queen Pictania trusted Tiernon implicitly and pulled down the bed covers to reveal the small babies. Delano stepped forward and sampled the air with his nose as he spoke, "These are the chosen ones. I will guard them with my life."

Queen Pictania was overjoyed. She said merrily. "I have the most powerful druid in the entire world for protection and the strongest beast. I am in safe hands."

Tiernon gave a look of joy and asked, "What will you name them, my Queen?"

She looked at him with a warm smile of affection on her face. "I will leave that honour to you. I am sure your choice will be a worthy one."

Tiernon was humbled. A tear came to his eyes and he made the same excuse as before. "There it is again; I have something in my eye."

He looked long and hard at the two babies before speaking. "I will name the boy Kael, for this means a mighty warrior and I will name the girl Breanna, for this means strong and virtuous."

Queen Pictania nodded in agreement. "That is a wise choice Tiernon. I knew I could rely on you."

*

As Shylah had promised, all was well in Brigantes. Crops were good, food was plenty and the clansmen and women were prosperous and peaceful.

Tiernon, Queen Pictania, the Pooka and the twins formed a tight bond. The Queen and her children were never far away from the protection of Tiernon or Delano. The twins had a happy childhood; they grew fast and were both walking, running and playing under the watchful eye and protection of the Pooka. Delano was a good friend to have. The twins would often play hide and seek with the Pooka. He had the power to disappear at will, so if the twins discovered his hiding spot he would trick them by fading away. Their favourite pastime was riding on his huge back when he was in wolf form. However, best of all was play fighting when he was in bear form. They would often play in the forest and pretend to hunt him down, jumping up and down on his belly once they had captured him.

Although Delano was playing, he was ever watchful of danger and always kept his wits about him. The twins, albeit very young, had already begun learning the ways of nobility, as the young children of a farmer would learn the art of farming and as the young children of a blacksmith would learn how to fashion iron. They would soon have to learn the art of weaponry and warfare, as did all children of the Celtic clans. They mostly enjoyed the time spent with their mother, Queen Pictania. She never tired of their company. Although it was not considered noble, the Queen would play games with them, tell stories to them and do all the things other mothers did. Tiernon was like the father they never knew. He kept them in their place, with the Queen's permission of course. One day he decided to show them his gift of thunder and burnt down a whole field of crops, much to the delight of the children, but the grown-ups were not very pleased.

The days passed quickly into weeks, months and years; the twins' third birthday was approaching fast. Tiernon's heart was growing sad because he knew it would soon be time to summon his sister, Shylah.

*

On the morning of the twins' third birthday, Tiernon made his way to the great river that flowed from the north. He went alone and his heart was heavy. He sang a chant and Shylah rose from the water. She did not look her usual self; her face was sombre and when she spoke her voice was quivered. She spoke slowly, "The day has arrived that I have most feared. I have grave news to tell you."

Tiernon looked older than ever. The weight of the whole world seemed to be on his shoulders. It was as if he already knew the answer to his question, but he asked it all the same. "What news do you have my sister? Have you foreseen the steps we must take to stop the changeling?"

She quivered as she replied and could not look Tiernon in the eye.

"As I have said before, only the sacrifice of one who is pure in heart can prevent the changeling from taking the twins."

She paused for a moment as if finding the right time to proceed. Tiernon was frustrated and said sharply. "Come on! Say it! Tell me!"

She replied sombrely, "There is nothing in this world purer than the love of a mother for her children. The mother must sacrifice herself and offer her life to the changeling in exchange for the life of her twins."

Tiernon stumbled backwards as if shot by an invisible arrow. He was clutching his chest as if his heart was bursting and his face was twisted in remorse as he struggled to speak. "This cannot be, not Pictania, my Queen and my friend, noooooooooooooooo."

He ran from the spot, heading in the direction of the fort. Shylah desperately wanted to follow him to stop him from going any further but alas, she could not escape the water as she was bound to stay there. She shouted for him to come back several times and even when he was out of sight she spoke through the power of her mind, but he blocked her out. She had something of great importance to tell him but he was too angered to listen and made his way in the direction of the Queen. His plan was to take her away, for he had become her closest friend. He never realised how deep his feelings ran until the news of today brought it all home to him. He was quite prepared to jeopardise the whole task to save her; so strong was his remorse at that moment.

He finally reached the Queen's chambers and what he saw there only compounded his pain. Queen Pictania was lying face down on the floor. Her dream regarding the changeling had reoccurred. She had already summoned Shylah the night before and knew what she must do. There was no doubt in her mind and she acted without hesitation in the early hours and took her own life.

*

Tiernon turned the Queen to face him and held her lovingly in his arms. She was clutching a long dagger handle. The blade was deep inside her, piercing the heart. Tiernon, overcome with remorse, had tears flowing freely down his face as he sobbed uncontrollably and loudly. He held the Queen for a long time before finding the power within him to regroup his emotions. He gathered the Queen up into his arms and carried her to the lake. The villagers rushed to him to enquire what had happened, but Tiernon snarled at everyone who came too close and threatened to strike dead anyone who interfered. Tiernon was a mighty druid and feared throughout the land. Everyone kept away, including his long-time friend, Delano the Pooka.

*

Tiernon finally reached the river where Shylah was already awaiting his arrival. He lifted the Queen aloft as if to show her to Shylah and spoke low yet with much anger, "You, who were once my sister yet are no more, kept this from me so that I could not save her. What have you to say for yourself before I strike you down?"

Shylah was quite frightened. Although she was an immortal spirit she knew that the wrath of Tiernon was powerful and in anger he could somehow find the way to kill her, so she replied in earnest, "I spoke to the Queen last night. She had seen once again the vision of the changeling and came to me in the twilight hours. She knew what she must do without my advice. She came to me and begged that I would not speak with you. Neither you nor I could have stopped her."

Tiernon just stared at Shylah and with venom in his voice he said, "You did not even try. You did not even care."

The anger that Tiernon showed to Shylah hurt her deeply and in defence she said, "We are of the old world. We both know that the Gods rule against evil. The Queen died willingly. If you had stopped her this morning, she would have taken her life this afternoon. The changeling is a dead soul, sent by the Evil One, which no one can kill. The Gods found a way to trick the changeling many years ago. Sacrifice is the only way. You know as well as I do that once the changeling comes for something then it must return with something. I loved the Queen as you did and I will miss her as you will. I am sorry my brother."

Tiernon placed the Queen gently to the ground and whispered in her ear. "I will not let you rot in the bowels of the earth with evil for company. When my quest is complete, I will return for your soul and take you from the place of no return and present you to the Gods. I will demand that they return you to your rightful place on this earth."

When Tiernon made a vow, he stuck to it.

*

Tiernon was a little calmer by now. He knew his place in the world and understood that honour bound him to do the bidding of the Gods. He looked up at Shylah and spoke with remorse,

31

"Please forgive me my sister, my heart is heavy and I spoke with evil from my mouth. Emotion overcame me. I know what I must do. Moreover, I will do it because of my word and bond as I have always done. I hope and pray that the chosen ones are worth it. I hope they can live up to all our expectations."

Shylah gave Tiernon a reassuring look as she replied, "I accept your apology. I know that it will be a long time before you recover from today. I know the pain that you carry and I know that we will never be the same again, but I love you brother."

With tears in her eyes and a heavy heart she disappeared into the water.

*

Later that day, Tiernon, Delano and the nobility held a mock funeral for the Queen. They could not bury her for she had to be kept for the changeling but the whole village from the large fort and the lower forts had gathered to pay their last respects. Although it was the day of Imbolc, the celebrations did not go ahead. The Queen, laid out in a white, silk gown looked restful and regal; her beauty shone even in death. A local woodsman had donated a finely crafted boat, in which the Queen lay, to aid her journey to the other side. The small vessel carved from a fallen oak tree, had all sorts of fine decorations including several forest creatures, each symbolising life and death.

The leader of the guard, Tiernon, and four of the Queen's soldiers gently carried the boat with its precious cargo to the marshes' edge. Once the procession had reached the place they lowered the boat to the ground and mourners began offering goblets and gold jewellery to the Gods. This was purely symbolic as the Queen had sacrificed herself to the changeling and could not pass over. Many well-wishers chanted prayers and all were sad.

*

After the service was over Tiernon and Delano took the Queen to the children's bedroom and laid her in their bed. They hid the children in one of the lower forts for safety. Tiernon knew the changeling would come after midnight, so he took the chance to see the Queen for one last time. He looked over her for a few moments and then bowed to his knees with his head held low as he spoke.

"I vow to you once more that when my journey is over, I will crawl down a hole in the ground until I reach the underworld. With all the power left in me, I will return you to your rightful place on Earth. Goodbye Queen."

He retired to his own quarters but did not sleep that night.

*

Shortly after midnight a skulking figure shone in the moonlight. It was swimming across the great river that ran from the north towards the marsh. It hauled itself out of the water and on to the marshy shore. In the shadows of the shrubs and marsh marigolds that grew quite tall the creature blended seamlessly. Occasionally the moonlight caught it and its green flesh shone. It was the changeling, a truly menacing, evil creature. It sneaked towards the large fort slowly and stealthily, stopping every time it heard the slightest rustle of a blade of grass. Finally it reached the great walls of the fort and scaled them with the ease and skill of a lizard. As it passed by the guard, although it was unseen, he felt a great shudder of cold and his hairs rose on the back of his neck; he knew that something dead was nearby. His complexion turned grey and he was truly afraid. The changeling arrived outside the children's bedchamber and as it opened the door to enter the room, it wore a menacing grin. This soon turned to sheer anger when it saw the Queen, for it knew it had been outsmarted. Unwillingly, the creature swooped the Queen into its arms and scuttled off back to the bowels of the underworld.

Chapter 5

The Early Years

Shortly after the Queen's death the nobles sent word to Alfred, the cousin of Cedric, for his help. He was the leader of the closely related Atrebates clan who were the second most powerful group in Southern Briton. They issued the use of coins and had many contacts with Gaul and Belgia and their territory stretched for over a hundred miles in all directions.

The ancestors of the Brigantes and Atrebates tribes had crossed the great sea together and taken residence in different parts of the country. Alfred was close to his cousin so the nobles from the Brigantes tribe were sure that he would come to their aid. They needed his help to rule the Brigantes tribe until the children were old enough and wise enough to take up the honour for themselves. Alfred was a great warrior; he was strong, wise, well versed in battle and well-travelled. He agreed to help immediately, leaving his eldest son to rule his own tribe. He travelled to Brigantes alone and when he met the children for the first time he took to them quickly. He saw the likeness in Breanna to the late Queen Pictania, and he saw the likeness in Kael to his late Cousin Cedric.

Tiernon confided in Alfred about the quest to come and gave him the responsibility of training the twins in the art of warfare, hunting and survival skills. He did his job well and trained them from that day forward. Although the twins were young, they were skilled with the sword, the axe, the bow and the long spear. Training often started at first light and continued well into the afternoon. At first they were trained to use wooden weapons but quickly moved on to the real article. On some days Alfred would take the twins out on great ponies to remote places. He would leave them with Delano for protection, but they were expected to find their own way home using the skills he had taught them. They would follow the position of the sun by day and the position of the stars by night. Surprisingly, given their age, they were able to feed off the land and hunt successfully for meat. Breanna was the best hunter. Her skill with the bow was excellent for a child so young and it was obvious that with age she would develop into a true master. Kael was a typical boy of his age, he would lose concentration easily, but Delano would quickly set him straight.

*

One time, whilst they were out on an expedition, Kael tried his hand at trapping. He dug a large pit in a clearing in the woods. It took him most of the morning and he did it alone. He hacked the hard ground with a digging tool. It was hard work. Once he had completed his excavation he sharpened some short sticks to a point and thrust them into the ground at the bottom of the pit. He covered the hole with tree branches woven tightly together and disguised them with earth. His job was completed with such expertise that the ground looked untouched and good enough to walk on. He followed a small stream back to camp and greeted his sister and Delano.

"I have set a worthy trap further downstream. I have seen a family of wild boar and feel confident that one of the young ones will stray into it. I am going back in the morning to check."

Breanna giggled loudly as she replied, "You will not catch a thing and I bet I could see your trap from a mile away!"

Kael scowled crossly, "You will not wish to share my meal tomorrow then, will you?"

Breanna took her bow in one hand and swiftly ran to the direction of the forest. A little further in the distance she stopped and turned towards Kael as she said jokingly, "And you will not wish to share the meal I am about to catch, will you?"

Breanna followed the stream that cut into the forest. She was heading for a small clearing that she had visited on many previous excursions. The forest was young and sparse; earlier settlers had cleared the land and the trees, which were just beginning to regain their hold. There were many silver birches growing tall, with hawthorn trees blossoming outward toward the sun. Young oak had begun to grow amongst the thick foliage and thorny protection, away from the hungry mouths of browsing deer.

Breanna followed a visible path that cut its way through the forest floor, meandering towards a clearing in the distance. As she got closer to the clearing she slowed her pace; crouching low, choosing her footing very carefully. Making sure that she did not rustle a single leaf, she took an arrow from her quiver and loaded her bow. She pulled the bowstring to her cheek and looked straight down the shaft. She had a large, male deer in her sights but before shooting she remembered the teachings of Alfred, that she should only kill what was necessary. She turned her sight to a small fawn. It was a twin. If she killed this one, the other would have the chance to survive; besides hunting was good and this would be plenty for the three of them. She let the bow fly and it whisked through the air straight into the heart of the young deer. The herd scampered away as the fawn dropped like a stone.

Later that night Breanna, Kael and Delano sat around the campfire enjoying the taste of young venison. Delano was a messy eater and slapped at his food as he spoke with a full mouth, "This meat is delicious. Thank goodness one of you can hunt."

He smiled as he winked towards Breanna. Kael replied angrily.

"So, you will not want your dinner tomorrow either?"

He scoffed. Breanna and Delano laughed aloud as he said, "You are like a fish, Kael, easy to reel in and quick to bite."

Kael picked at a bone to get the last morsels of meat with juice running down his chin. He saw the funny side and began laughing himself. A while after his hearty meal had settled Kael lay on the floor, looking thoughtfully into the night sky as he spoke to Delano, "Do you think the Gods can see me now?"

Delano pondered a moment before answering. Kael was keen to hear what he had to say and began to fidget. Delano said, "The Gods have watched you since before you were born. They instructed Tiernon to guard and protect you."

Kael had an inquisitive mind and wanted to know everything. He asked another question. "Why are we the chosen ones?"

Delano pondered a moment before he answered. "I do not know why you are the chosen ones. I only know that according to prophecy you must be, you were born at the right time. All the events leading up to your birth fulfilled the prophecy."

Kael interrupted with yet another question, "What if we are not the chosen ones?"

This question disturbed Delano, "I hope that you are. We have invested a lot of time in the two of you. People have given their lives for this cause. I would not want to imagine that you were anything but the chosen."

Kael looked troubled as he asked, "Did our mother die so that we could live? I wish it was not so, I hate the past; I wish I could forget it all."

Delano replied softly, "When you are older and wiser you will understand. Please do not ask any more questions. We need to get some rest as we have a long day ahead of us tomorrow."

*

Early the next morning Kael was the first to rise. He was eager to visit the pit that he had dug the previous day to see if he had caught a worthy meal. He ran quickly towards the pit and discovered that it had been disturbed. He was a little puzzled because someone or something had covered it up again but not well enough, because he could see the disturbance on the ground. Cautiously, he uncovered the pit and to his total surprise there was a hobgoblin sat at the bottom. Somehow it had missed every single spike in the ground. It looked up at him and spoke, "Are you going to eat me?"

Kael fell back to his bottom in fits of laughter and replied, "I cannot eat you, for your kind taste of rotting fish. I will keep you for a pet. I have been after one of your kind for ages and I hear tell that you make a worthy companion."

The hobgoblin looked relieved as it said, "Then, I thank you for providing me with the perfect hiding place. You saved my life last night."

Kael climbed back to his feet with a bemused look on his face as he asked, "How do you mean? Those spikes could have killed you."

The hobgoblin giggled loudly and said, "I did not fall down here. I could see that this was a trap from a mile away. I climbed down here to escape a bear. He chased me right to the edge. Even the bear knew it was a trap. Once he realised that he could not get to me safely, he tried to cover the pit back up."

Kael was very displeased. He threw down a large log that was on the ground nearby as he responded dismayingly, "Here, climb this, I will take you back to camp and I will let you live but on one condition."

The hobgoblin replied inquisitively, "What condition?"

Kael whispered something in his ear then took him quickly to camp. Breanna was awake; Delano had gone off to fetch fresh water.

Kael bragged, "Look what I have caught."

He nudged the hobgoblin as he said, "Tell her how I caught you."

The hobgoblin looked sheepish as he replied, "I was wandering through the woods looking for food. I walked into the clearing and before I knew it, I was down the hole. It was a wonder that I missed the spikes; I did not know what had happened. This trap was the best I had ever seen."

Kael was visibly grinning from ear to ear. Breanna looked shocked as she said to the hobgoblin, "You did not have a notion that the trap was there?"

The hobgoblin stuttered his answer, "Not at all, this was a good trap."

The hobgoblin turned to Kael with a wink and whispered, "Will that do, Sire?"

Kael quickly hushed the hobgoblin just as Delano walked into camp with skins brimming with water. Delano eyed the hobgoblin with suspicion, for he knew that if treated kindly these creatures made good servants, but treated mean they made worse enemies. He questioned the creature, "Where do you come from little one?"

The hobgoblin eyed Delano with equal distrust, for he also knew that a Pooka could be a rather troublesome beast. He replied with truth as he dared not to differ, "I come from a small local tribe a few miles west of here. I recently escaped my old master and was returning to my village."

Delano threw another question at him, "Why have you left your master?"

The hobgoblin replied, "He treated me roughly. My first master was kind and I worked hard, but when he died his son became my owner and he beat me."

Delano gave a look of mistrust as he asked another question, "I know well the tales told of an ill-treated hobgoblin. What was your punishment to your mean master before leaving?"

The hobgoblin thought hard about what to say, but knowing the ways of a Pooka he felt it best to answer truthfully.

"I stole all his animals and drove them over a cliff."

Kael looked positively angered and was about to strike the creature, but Delano grabbed him firmly by the arm and warned him sharply, "Think long and hard, boy, before taking this creature as your servant and remember this. Never strike a hobgoblin, for in doing so you will make yourself the worst enemy you can imagine. Always treat this creature with kindness and you will not give it cause to grieve you. I warn you now, if you feel in your heart that you will one day treat this creature with less than good will, then let him go today."

Kael was lost for words and was not sure what to do next. The hobgoblin looked at Kael with sympathetic eyes and said, "If it pleases you, Sire, I will not do another wrong to my old master."

Kael looked pleased as he asked. "It would please me very much. Do you have a name?"

The hobgoblin replied with a doleful smile, "My name is Vaughan."

Kael gestured towards his friends with a happy grin as he said, "Then please meet my worthy sister, Breanna, my faithful guard and honourable friend, Delano and I am Kael."

He then looked at the hobgoblin as he asked, "If I treat you with kindness, do you promise to serve me with kindness and can I trust you, always?"

The hobgoblin grinned and gave a swift response, "Always sire, always. Will you please take me with you? You have a kind spirit."

Kael agreed and Delano shook his head. Vaughan ran around in circles, singing with joy. He then ran off into the woods and gathered all the wood he could carry, talking to himself all the while. He came scurrying back with arms laden with wood and laid them out ready to make a fire. As he did so, he began to tell the trio enthusiastically how useful he could be. "I can make fire, I can hunt, I can track and I can stay awake for days on end. I can cook, I am a good listener and I can give advice. I can sing, dance and make beer."

The trio looked around at each other wondering when Vaughan would stop long enough to take a breath. Kael said jokingly to Delano, "I know what you meant now. I have known the beast for a few moments and already I want to strangle him."

They all erupted in fits of laughter.

Vaughan could tell that he was only jesting and replied whilst giggling, "If you were to strangle me now sire you would surely miss all the other wonderful things I could do. I can climb trees, I can fetch, I can carry and I can talk and talk and talk."

Vaughan fell about laughing, joined by the rest of the group and then jumped in with another remark, "Did I tell you I can live for three hundred years? You have to put up with me for a long, long time."

By now they were all in hysterics of laughter and chuckled for a good few minutes until the loud crack of a twig caught the sensitive ear of Delano and his laughter halted. He looked in the direction of the noise and spied a large brown coloured bear in full charge, heading towards the camp. It was almost upon them. Delano had no time to utter a word of warning but said aloud to himself, "Change."

He transformed into a huge bear and lunged towards the large intruder, which now seamed dwarfed by comparison and they crashed together in a fierce clinch. Delano came off the worse for he had no time to brace the force. The brown bear was astride him and began slashing at his face. Breanna was the next to realise what was happening and began scrambling around in search of her bow. Kael jumped to his feet and began fidgeting for his sword. Surprisingly, Vaughan was the quickest to act. He took a large stick from the pile of wood that he had gathered earlier and scampered with the speed of a hare towards the fighting duo. He pounced on the brown bear's back and scampered up to its shoulders. Swinging the stick as hard as he could, he smacked the bear clean between the eyes. The bear turned quickly, throwing Vaughan to the floor. Breanna had now found her bow and let an arrow fly clean into the bear's arm and Kael slashed bravely with his sword towards the bear's face. Delano was now on his feet again. He quickly regained his composure and lunged towards the brown bear and with several massive swipes to the bear's face he managed to scare it into submission. The bear quickly retreated into the woods and was gone. Delano returned to his usual human like form and stared at Vaughan who was back on his feet, shaking his head from side to side to regain his consciousness. Delano held out his hand to shake Vaughan's hand in friendship. "You failed to mention you could fight, brave one. I thank you. I am your friend for life."

Vaughan took his hand quickly. He was overjoyed that Delano had recognised his bravery and much more overjoyed that he had honoured him with a handshake. This was the beginning of a long friendship between the four brave warriors.

Chapter 6

The Journey Begins

The years passed quickly and it was not long before the twins were approaching their thirteenth season. Shylah, with the power of thought, summoned Tiernon to the river for council. She rose from the water a few feet away from her brother.

Time had been good to her; she did not look a day older and was as beautiful as ever. She gazed at Tiernon with troubled eyes as she spoke to him, "The time is drawing nearer for the children to begin their journey. It is only three days to their birthday and they must prepare and be ready to set off on that day before the sun rises. There must be no celebrations and no talk to anyone but Delano and the children."

Tiernon looked stern as he asked, "Are the evil doers aware that the time is near to begin our quest?"

Shylah looked all knowing as she replied, "They are indeed. It is prophesied that they will do all that they can to blight our progress. We have time on our side. If we cancel the celebrations we will be able to begin the journey a day early."

Tiernon liked the plan. However, he had one concern, so he asked, "I believe that this would arouse unnecessary suspicion. I think it would be wise to go ahead with the festivities as normal. That way we can sneak away in the early hours. No one will suspect a thing if they believe we are to attend the feast."

Shylah looked positively delighted as she replied, "How wise you are my brother. What a cunning plan."

Tiernon clapped his hands together in quick succession, as if rewarding his own intelligence as he spoke on, "I will ask Vaughan to pack a good pony and cart with food and weapons."

Shylah looked shocked by this remark and was quick to retort, "That cannot be. Vaughan must not know about this; he has a loose tongue. He cannot go on this journey."

Tiernon appeared saddened by this news as he debated, "That is a pity. Vaughan has become a great friend to the children. They will miss him dearly. He could be useful to us."

Shylah disagreed profusely and proceeded to instruct Tiernon on the finer details of the journey and she spoke of the direction they must take. Tiernon later collaborated with his companions about the details and together they carefully laid their plans.

*

The days passed quickly and on the eve before Imbolc, Tiernon made his way quietly to the stable to make ready a stout pony and strong cart. He rushed to the pony shelter that lay just inside the large fort. He was surprised to see that Vaughan was already saddling a large well-rounded pony to a cart. Vaughan took one look at Tiernon and said, "I am sorry Tiernon. I was not intending to hear your conversation with the great Shylah. However, I was in a position whereby not hearing you was almost impossible. Now that I do know of your plans you will not stop me. I will go with you and I promise I will not speak a word of it to anyone, not a living soul."

Tiernon eyed the hobgoblin with a mixture of emotions, angry yet simultaneously pleased. It did not take him long before he found himself embracing the hobgoblin and welcoming him aboard. The twins were in their bedchamber. They could not sleep because of their sheer excitement at the prospect of embarking on a great adventure. That was the way they viewed the whole affair. The adults were extremely serious about it, but to them it was a chance to explore and have fun. They chatted into the early hours, all the while Delano held a vigil outside their room guarding against unwanted visitors. Tiernon suddenly but quietly entered the room.

"It is time. I have a cart waiting outside. We must journey south, as fast and as far as we can, before the day breaks. Are you ready?"

The twins pulled down their bed covers and they were both in full dress. Breanna had her trusty bow and dagger at her side and Kael waved his short Celtic sword in the air. They looked at each other and said simultaneously, "This is what we were born to do."

The trio headed off in the direction of the stable. Delano was now with Vaughan and ready for the journey. He needed no weapons. Vaughan produced two sacks, one filled with dried goat's meat and the other with oat biscuits. He said, "I have prepared these in case the hunting is bad. There is about three days' worth of food here and it should keep us going until we are of a safe distance away, before we can begin hunting and cooking."

Tiernon was pleased. He looked at Vaughan and said warmly, "I am glad I allowed you to come even though it is forbidden. I feel that you will be an asset to the group."

Vaughan was very happy; he loved praises. The cart was laden with all sorts of other goods including cooking utensils, weapons, clothing, money, flour and salt. Before the group set off in the cart, which was incredibly noisy on the track, Tiernon began to chant in a language that the others did not comprehend. He was casting one of his many Brichts (magic spells) on the village and the surrounding forts. It was a sleeping spell that made every one fall into a deep slumber. A strange wind whistled about the place, drifting from dwelling to dwelling. Upon reaching each person in their beds, they murmured and fell into deeper sleep. Tiernon addressed the group, "We are ready to go. I just need to take care of the lookout. I have left him awake to protect the village."

The group set off out of the stable and towards the fort gates. The wheels made a loud grinding noise on the hard soil and a squeaking that resonated loudly due to the stillness of the night. The night lookout was soon up on his feet and put his horn quickly to his lips as if to raise the alarm, when suddenly Tiernon cast a mind spell which possessed the watchman. With the powers of suggestion the lookout opened the gates and let the band continue their journey without harassment.

When the trio reached the other side of the gates and out into the open Tiernon made one more suggestion. "Close the gate."

The lookout closed the gates behind them and once the group was a safe distance away he returned to his normal self and the deep sleep spell was lifted from the village.

*

The group followed the great river that ran from the north and proceeded in a southerly direction with the dark forest on their right. When they reached a spot where the river was shallow enough to cross, they made their way to the other side and disappeared amongst the foliage of the forest.

Once in the forest Tiernon reached into his robe and pulled out a large banner made of the finest cloth, bound neatly and skilfully to a carved wooden pole. He unravelled it to reveal a tapestry of the emblem of the White Bear and addressed the group,

"This banner is the symbol of hope and new beginnings. It will offer us safe journey through any fort and any tribe that follow the ways of the Gods. Without it, we may fall into battle every time that we pass a village or a stranger."

Breanna stared at the banner as Tiernon slotted the pole into the holder on the front of the cart. It wafted in the wind and the White Bear emblem seemed as if it was flying in the breeze. She quizzed, "It is beautiful. Did you make it Tiernon?"

He paused briefly for a moment as if reminiscing about times gone by, as he answered, "It was made by your mother's hands. She said it would bring us luck and I hope it will."

Breanna was in awe. It made her feel special to learn that her late mother had made something on her behalf. She was happy and sat quietly with her own thoughts whilst the others chatted about the journey. Suddenly, Delano pricked up his ears. He had picked up the smell of a group of many unearthly creatures lurking deeper in the forest and began scanning the area with his ears to pinpoint the culprits. He nudged Vaughan and whispered, "There are quite a few of your kind out tonight. I can smell them."

Vaughan looked back at Delano with a cheeky grin as he replied, "They can probably smell you as well. Phew what an odour!"

Delano grinned. The pair had become great friends over the years. Vaughan, although joking, would never have been so bold on their first meeting all those years ago.

*

Night past into early morning and a red sun began to edge its way into the sky. The trees cast eerie shadows on the forest floor and the group became aware that they were been followed by a mob of hobgoblins. Kael sat up anxiously, but Vaughan quickly put him at ease.

"Do not worry yourself sire; they are my friends. They have aided our way through the dark woods, keeping other foul creatures at bay."

Tiernon became aware that Vaughan must have told his friends of the time they meant to embark and he scowled at Vaughan as he spoke, "Shylah was right when she said you have a loose tongue. When did you tell all your friends that we were leaving?"

Vaughan looked back rather sheepishly and gave a quivering answer, "Honest, master Tiernon, I only told my closest friends. I thought it would be good for us to have safe passage through the first night and I meant no harm."

Tiernon could never stay angry at Vaughan for very long as he always meant well, so he put him at ease. "No harm done. I thank your friends for their protection."

Vaughan requested permission to set up camp with the hobgoblins. When Tiernon granted his wish he was over the moon and wasted no time at all in calling his friends to join the group. He knew that the journey would be a dangerous one and that this may be his last chance to speak with his own kind. Delano transformed himself into a large, black eagle and patrolled the surrounding area to make sure that they were not in any danger. He returned with the all clear and the group tucked into dried goat's meat and oat biscuits. The hobgoblins were happy to sit and talk. They had already feasted on several creepy crawlies that lurked within the forest in the night hours.

One of the hobgoblins spoke up, "As you venture further south, a few days travel from here, before you reach the vast moorland, you will come across a small settlement in the woods. There you will find more of our people. The leader of the group goes by the name of Demetae. He will offer you food, drink and safe haven so that you may gather your strength before the huge moor crossing".

Vaughan looked pleased with himself. He knew that his actions were honourable and that his friends would look on him favourably because of the helpfulness shown to them by his kin. The hobgoblin that had just spoken was Vaughan's uncle, Conrad. He was famous in the world of the goblins; never serving any master. On several occasions he was reputed to have joined forces with the indigenous men folk in battles against the Celts, when they encountered them during their early invasions.

He was renowned for his battle tactics. Stories of old are still told by those that remember of how he evaded capture by hiding in the caves and holes in the ground, which were the gateways to the underworld. It was often said that he had ventured deep into the earth's bowels and seen things that no earthly creature or being had seen ever before and lived to tell the tale. Vaughan was proud of his heritage. He entertained the others by reciting poems that were written long ago in honour of his uncle.

Upon hearing that Conrad had succeeded in navigating the earth's depths, Tiernon's eyes widened with excitement as he spoke, "I am interested to know more of your excursions to the underworld. When this task is done I would like to meet with you again as I have a promise to keep and may require your services, if you are willing."

Conrad replied enthusiastically, "Any friend of my nephew is a friend of mine. I will be honoured to help you."

The pair were happy. A hobgoblin never broke his word. Tiernon slept well that night.

*

The next day Breanna and Kael were the first to rise. They quickly packed their blankets into the cart and set off on foot in search of something good to eat for breakfast. They came across a wild crab apple tree and climbed it to get to the best fruits. From the uppermost branches Breanna could see the rest of the forest, which stretched far out towards the horizon.

Taken aback by the sight, she spoke to her brother, "I cannot see an end to the trees and it looks as though we will never reach the other side".

Kael reassured his sister, "Do not worry Breanna. It seems like a long way, but we will make it. Do not become disheartened so early in our quest."

Breanna returned a stern glance towards her brother as she scoffed, "I am not worried, I was merely thinking aloud. Do you want an apple?"

She tossed an apple swiftly towards Kael and it caught him clean at the side of his face, almost uprooting him from his perch. An apple throwing fight quickly ensued. At first it were in anger, but the pair were soon in fits of laughter. Kael spotted something on the ground and suddenly stopped throwing apples. But Breanna had not yet noticed the figure standing at the foot of the tree and continued the fight, catching Kael unaware with another clean strike to his face. He turned to her with a surprised look as if trying to warn her to stop. He made head gestures to cast her attention to where he was looking but she paid no heed and threw yet another apple.

Suddenly and loudly a voice thundered out, "Why don't you just blow a horn as loud as you can and announce your whereabouts to the whole world?"

Breanna looked in the direction of the voice and she froze on the spot. Tiernon stood at the base of the tree with his arms folded to confirm his anger. He spoke again, this time a little softer. "Come down at once you foolish children."

They scuttled quickly to the ground with lots of apples falling from within their tartan shirts. One plopped on to Tiernon's head, which only made matters worse. Upon reaching the ground the pair rushed past Tiernon and headed back to camp, but not before he gave them both a scorning slap on the back of their heads. Tiernon, shaking his head, gathered as many apples as he could carry. It would be a shame to waste such a prize.

*

Shortly after their breakfast the group said their goodbyes to the hobgoblins and set off on the long journey south, following an ancient ancestral pathway which meandered through the age-old woodland. As promised by Conrad, the travellers arrived at the settlement of the hobgoblins, set on the fringes of the great forest. Their living quarters were simple earthen mounds dug into the natural hillsides that were dotted about close together, rather like large badger sets. Tiernon halted the cart and proceeded on foot, taking with him the banner of the White Bear. He indicated for the rest to stay in the cart whilst he surveyed the area. It was not long before a well-rounded hobgoblin appeared to greet him. He recognised the hobgoblin immediately through the description given by Conrad. It was Demetae.

"Welcome to my home. You must be Tiernon the mighty. Your reputation precedes you."

Tiernon looked rather pleased as he responded, "I thank you for your kindness. I will return the favour someday."

*

The group settled down for the next few days setting up camp under skins that were graciously provided by the hobgoblins. Vaughan was in his element and shared stories with his relatives about the times of old when their kind ruled the earth, before the onset of men. The twins also swapped stories with the young hobgoblins and Breanna took the time to show them how she made her fine bow from the best yew wood. They all took turns shooting at targets and the time spent there was a happy one.

Chapter 7

The Gabriel Hounds

The days passed quickly and the group said their farewells and began their long trek across the harsh moorland. This was a barren wasteland filled with hidden bogs and swamps. The occasional rowan tree grew in solitary defiance and the grass was present in abundance, mingled with heather, which was a good source of nourishment. It was a dangerous landscape; the group was at the mercy of the enemy with little or no place to hide. Many a foul creature roamed in this hostile land.

It was not always this way. It was once a lush green forest, vibrant with life, before the early settlers had uplifted all the trees to clear the land for farming, only to retreat years later once the land around them became infertile.

Tiernon turned towards his party, "We must all stay alert. This land is vast and evil rules this area. There are many dangers to look out for."

Delano transformed into a great black eagle and scoured the area and it was not long before he returned with a stern look about him. He spoke in a troubled voice, "I have seen a large pack of hungry dogs heading in our direction, sniffing the earth as if on the trail of some prey. They do not look as if they are from this world."

Tiernon looked all-knowing as he informed the group, "They must be the Gabriel hounds! Ghostly dogs that once lived, but have since turned to decay, conjured by the Evil One and cast upon the earth to roam eternally in the search for human flesh. We must use all our stealth and guile to try and stay out of their way."

Kael drew his short sword from his scabbard as he said defiantly, "I am not afraid, let them come!"

Tiernon gave an angry glance as he scolded, "Put your sword away. It is useless against them. No man-made weapon can harm a single hair on their heads. Many years ago I heard a tale that the Gabriel hounds ripped to shreds an entire Celtic army that was on a reconnaissance march. There was nothing they could do to defend themselves and everyone died, ravaged and savaged and eventually eaten, bones and all."

The twins simply stared at each other with fright. Vaughan shuddered from head to toe and Delano showed fear for the first time in his entire life. The group was transfixed in sombre thought when suddenly Vaughan broke the silence. "If it pleases you, may I make a suggestion?"

Tiernon looked up as if awoken from deep thoughts and responded expectantly, "Any plan at this hour would be a good one. What is your proposal?"

Vaughan mused over his thoughts as he replied, "I think we should split into three. Delano could head towards the hounds in wolf form and encourage them to follow his trail. If he was to get too close to the hounds he could change into an eagle and fly away. Meanwhile, I could set my own trail in another direction, should he fail. You could escape with the twins to the south and if the God's are willing, we could all meet up again later once we have shaken off the hounds".

Tiernon turned towards Delano as he questioned, "It does sound like a competent plan. Would you be willing to risk it?"

Delano took no time in responding as he slapped the hobgoblin heartily between the shoulder blades, "I would be honoured. Just when I thought I knew everything about a hobgoblin you always amaze me with something new. You are a brave, loyal and wise friend. Let's try it."

Vaughan had a grin which was positively brimming from ear to ear. He loved praise.

*

The team carefully finalised their plans and Delano was the first to set off. He transformed into the large black wolf and headed straight into the direction of the hounds. Vaughan quickly ran the other way towards the east, whilst Tiernon and the twins led their cart southward.

The cart trundled slowly on, for what seemed like an age. All the while the trio held their tongues, anxiously scouring the area in anticipation of a sudden attack of hounds.

Delano proceeded onwards and it was not long before he caught his first glimpse of the pack. There were around fifty or more of the beasts, tearing across the grassland at great speed. The sheer size of each hound was enough to astound him. He was not small himself yet they were almost equal in stature. Every dog was identical to the next as if spawned from a single mother. Their eyes were evil and red. Their bodies were hairy and their skin hung from the muscles like rotting corpses that had come back to life again. They had large, pointed ears and square features, ever snarling and extremely menacing. So transfixed was Delano on the pack that he ran headlong into a lone scout that instantly ravaged at his flesh, without warning and without mercy. Delano howled in pain and the rest of the pack came running towards him.

*

The twins heard the screams of pain in the distance and Breanna cried, "Oh no! Delano has been caught. They are killing him."

Tiernon was saddened. He knew that there was nothing he could do, for his task on this quest was to take care of the twins. Although he desperately wanted to help his friend he knew that he must proceed southward.

They ventured on to the cacophony of screams, howls and snarls coming from the distance until suddenly it stopped and everything fell silent again. Breanna and Kael buried their faces in their hands, sobbing uncontrollably. Through tears and staggered breath, Kael whimpered, "He is dead! He is dead! We should have tried to help him."

Tiernon was fighting back the tears and his eyes were burning and red as he scorned, "This day is the day for you to grow up. You must realise this day that we may all die in our quest. Take heed you foolish children and understand that you must never ever put yourselves in danger for us. We are merely the tools to get you where you are going."

The twins fell silent in their sadness and the trio journeyed onwards on the trundling cart. Fear had left them, replaced by utter remorse.

*

A small figure appeared over the brow of a large hill, approaching from the east. Running as fast as his legs could take him. Vaughan was shouting at the top of his voice, "Run! Flee for your lives, the beasts are upon us."

Vaughan was scampering towards the cart until eventually he was beside the trio. He overtook the pony and cart and was off into the distance.

Breanna turned her head towards the direction that Vaughan had run from to see a huge ball of dust on the brow of the hill and she could hear the thunder of many four-footed beasts as they drew ever closer. She saw them galloping down the slope with the speed of the wind and her heart leapt into her mouth. She knew instantly that the cart was no match in speed for the oncoming pack so she jumped to the ground and ran as fast as she could in the direction that Vaughan had taken. Kael had the same idea but ran in a direction of his own, away from the others. Tiernon left the cart and stood his ground, awaiting his fate. The pony bolted away, cart and all, with a new found speed, its eyes rolling wildly in its head. Upon seeing their prey run in all directions the pack of hungry hounds were baffled for a second but soon decided to go for the largest and weakest member of the group. They descended quickly and without mercy towards the pony, laden with a heavy cart, and wasted no time in disembowelling the stricken beast, ripping and tearing it limb from limb. Tiernon saw a chance to flee. He was going to stand and fight but thought better of it once he saw the pack squabbling and fighting for the morsels of the stricken pony. On and on he ran. He could see Breanna and Vaughan to the front of him, but Kael was running blindly in the wrong direction. Tiernon tried frantically to coerce Kael to run towards the others, but it was in vain. Kael was so gripped with fear that he just kept going the wrong way. The pack of hounds continued to fight and squabble over their new victim until there was nothing left but clean white bones. They did not stop there, they even ate the bones. This gave the trio ample time to get a good distance away, but not a safe one. The hounds circled around, sniffed the ground to find the scent trails, and stopped on the trails that lead to Kael. Vigilantly and swiftly they ran towards the boy.

*

Kael had been running for some time now and his heart was about to burst. Sweat was flowing down his face and he could suddenly hear the rumble of the beasts as they drew ever closer. He continued in vain as they closed in on him and at one point he could feel their breath on the back of his neck. Aimlessly and pointlessly he ran on all the same, wondering when he would feel the first deathblow.

Then he felt a sharp pain in both shoulders. Through fear and determination he carried on running although the pain was relentless. All the while the hounds were hot on his trail. His legs continued to pump and he felt like he was running on fresh air, but still he ran and ran with his eyes tight shut. The pain in his shoulders was still burning away and he felt that his life was leaving him, for he now had the feeling of flying. But still he ran and still the pain would not leave him. Suddenly, he heard a voice that he recognised. "Open your eyes, you are safe."

He found the strength to open his eyes and was surprised to see the pack of hounds far beneath him on the ground, leaping angrily and snarling, trying to reach him. He was baffled; how did he get so high? Why could he still feel the pain in his shoulders? He looked at his shoulders to see that there were two large black talons clutching him tightly. He looked skyward to see a large black eagle soaring on effortless wings. He then got a look at its face and noticed two beautiful piercing blue eyes and he spoke with glee. "Delano! You are alive. You are alive. I cannot believe that you are here and you saved me."

Kael laughed with a newfound joy, forgetting everything, even the pain in his shoulders. He was alive and he just smiled as Delano carried him far away.

Delano crossed over many fields and many rivers and eventually dropped Kael off in the watchtower of an old fort weathered by the winds of time and abandoned many years ago. "Stay here and stay quiet. I must try and save the others," Delano ordered.

Suddenly Kael's joy turned to sadness with the realisation that his sister and close friends were still at the mercy of the Gabriel hounds. Before he could utter one word, Delano was gone.

*

The hounds were now hot on the trail of Tiernon and the others, annoyed at losing one victim, but steadfast in their pursuit of the rest. Tiernon turned around quickly and could see the pack advancing swiftly towards him. He had now re-joined Breanna and Vaughan. The tired little hobgoblin simply could not run anymore and just fell to the ground in a heap of exhaustion.

Tiernon had to think quickly and without hesitation shouted to Breanna. "Get down on the ground!"

Breanna instantly fell to the ground alongside Vaughan. Although frightened, she trusted Tiernon with her life and knew that he must have a cunning plan. Tiernon spoke hastily as the hounds drew nearer, "With the power given to me by my father, give me the strength to prevail."

As quickly as the last words left his mouth Tiernon held his arms outwards towards the oncoming evil and two massive bolts of lightning instantly streamed towards the ground that separated the beasts from their prey. The earth cracked like a walnut, revealing a large deep chasm. So fast were the beasts approaching and so swift was the actions of the mighty Tiernon that the hounds had no time to stop. Some of the hounds fell blindly into the depths of the earth from whence they had come. Others tried in vain to halt, planting their legs firm in the ground. The beasts that ran behind them knocked them over the edge and into the vast chasm until all disappeared amongst lots of dust and loud wailing and howling, deeper into the depths until they could be heard no more.

Tiernon collapsed to the ground, exhausted. Never had he conjured up so much of his life's energy and he fell into unconsciousness.

Chapter 8

Destiny Revealed

Delano mustered up every ounce of his drained strength in search for his friends. As he circled the skies in weary exploration, he looked down at his legs that were in tatters and badly bleeding after he had survived a fierce battle with the hounds. Hopelessly outnumbered, he had endured many painful bites until he found the chance to turn from the wolf into the bear. With one mighty thrust of his huge paw he managed to bowl the hound dogs over. He lashed out repeatedly, knocking the hound dogs from left to right, until the opportunity arose for him to transform into the eagle and fly away to safety.

*

After a small respite he found the strength to save Kael, but there was still no time to think about the pain as his search went on. He eventually caught sight of the lonely cart. Equipment lay strewn about and sacks were tattered and torn. Delano feared the worse. He thought that his friends had met with the same fate as the pony. He searched on, circling around wearily in desperation until he spied a billow of smoke rising into the sky.

Vaughan had fortunately witnessed the eagle fly away to safety with Kael. He knew instantly that it was his old friend Delano so he made a small fire that was not effective until he covered it with wet moss, which crackled in the heat and gave off the steaming smoke.

Delano landed on the ground nearby and as he returned to his Pooka form, he collapsed through sheer exhaustion. Vaughan took one look at him and bowed his head in sorrow as he spoke to

Breanna, "I fear he has lost much blood. There does not seem to be a single place on his body that has not been bitten."

Breanna was beside herself with worry. Vaughan spoke, this time with a glint in his eye, "I have got an idea but you must stay here until I get back."

Breanna questioned apprehensively, "Where are you going?"

Vaughan giggled loudly as he looked towards Breanna with reassurance, "I am going to get the help of the fairy folk. They are everywhere, in the forest, in the sky and on the moors. You just need to know where to look and what to say when you find them. I will not be long."

Vaughan scuttled off heading towards the marshy bogs. He was like a fox sniffing out a hare, checking every nook and every cranny until he came to a small hole. To the human eye it was just a mouse hole, but Vaughan knew better. He put his mouth to the hole and whispered, "I am a small hobgoblin walking round and round. I need some great assistance oh fairies in the ground. Conquentae – opeouphus – meteouphus – arlum."

He sat for a few seconds by the hole. He was sure that it was a fairy home. Patiently he waited until at last appeared a tiny boy, who emerged cautiously into the open, stretching his arms and fluttering his wings. He spoke in anger, "What do you want goblin? How do you know the code?"

Vaughan smiled, "How I know the code, oh fairy, is no concern of yours, but I know that you are bound by fairy law to grant one wish to the code bearer."

Fairies were nasty creatures known to all for their mischief. They would often lead weary travellers off the track and into their homes to make them disappear forever.

The tiny, winged boy scurried back into the hole. After a few moments a large procession of fairies began emerging into the open, and not just from that hole but from under rocks, out behind blades of grass and out of the sky until a large crowd surrounded Vaughan. The queen of the fairies fluttered to the ground beside him. She was dressed in green and wore a purple hat. This was perfect camouflage for the heather where she lived. Her wings were like those of a dragonfly, delicate and silky.

She was angered that a hobgoblin knew the secret code so she spoke sternly, "State your business and say it quickly. You have one wish. Do not waste it."

Vaughan had to think long and hard. He began working it out on his fingers with his tongue sticking out whilst mumbling, "To save Tiernon, that's one wish. To save Breanna would take two wishes."

The fairy queen interrupted rudely, "You have only one wish."

Vaughan eyed her suspiciously and said disparagingly, "Please do not rush me."

He continued to do his sums until finally he spoke again, "I wish for you to grant me the one wish of ten wishes."

The fairy queen was furious and she was shaking her head with annoyance as she shouted angrily, "You cannot wish for ten wishes, which would be nine too many."

Vaughan tried many combinations in order to get the queen to agree, but no matter how he tried it always came back to the same answer. One wish. The fairy queen was anxious to get about her own business. Eventually she said, "Take me to your friends."

Vaughan led the fairy queen, escorted by the endless mob of fairies, to where Breanna was resting. Nearby Delano and Tiernon lay motionless. Breanna was in awe when she saw the fairies. She thought, like all children, that fairies were kind spirits.

Vaughan quickly warned her. "Do not trust these people. Keep your tongue in your mouth and your wits about you."

The fairy queen assessed the situation. She wanted to sort the matter quickly and get away from this foolish, annoying hobgoblin. She rubbed her chin whilst she mused, "This Pooka is injured. If I am correct, he must sleep until the moon appears before his wounds can heal."

The fairy knew the ways of a Pooka, the shape shifter. They had the ability to regenerate limbs and heal severe wounds but needed the power of the moon to do so.

Vaughan spoke up, "You can see my dilemma. I need to get everyone to a safe place and off the moors. I dare not wait till Delano wakes up, for the Gods only know what evil will turn up next."

The fairy queen thought a little longer before advising, "If I grant you the one wish and heal the Pooka, he could help you get the rest of your friends to safety."

Vaughan thought long and hard before he answered delightfully, "I agree. That is my wish. Heal Delano in the blink of an eye."

The fairy queen disappeared down a hole and returned with a small glass vial which contained a secret potion. She poured a single drop on the lips of Delano and said scornfully, "It is done. Now be off with you before I lose my temper."

She flapped her wings, rose into the air and flew back towards her home, followed by a swirling mass of her fairy minions, who buzzed about like a swarm of angry bees. One by one they disappeared without a trace and all was silent again.

Delano awoke fully regenerated but very groggy. His wounds healed before his eyes until eventually they disappeared. His energy returned as it was before the attack and at last he was fully recovered. Vaughan gave him a little time before explaining what had just happened and then laid down his plan.

"I need you to change into your horse form so that I can harness you to the cart. We could use it to carry Breanna and Tiernon to where you have taken Kael. I saw you save him."

Delano agreed; it was their only option. They loaded the cart with every salvageable possession that they could find, including Tiernon's treasured banner that was strewn, undamaged, on the ground and made their way towards the old fort.

It was a long journey and took them the rest of the day, reaching their destination when the moon was high in the sky. Kael spotted them from the watchtower and he was ecstatic.

*

The days grew wearily on, yet Tiernon lay in a state of delirium. Delano realised that his old friend had a weakness that he had never witnessed before. Tiernon drew strength from his life force when making thunder. The greater the force of thunder, the more life force he used.

As the group went about their daily routines keeping watch and caring for Tiernon, they were unaware that something strange and unearthly had happened to him. By the will of the creator himself, his soul was lifted from his body, which lay limp and lifeless like an empty shell. He was dead. His soul was carried high into the earthly sky and beyond. Into the open universe. Through fields of stars, black holes and into oblivion, until reaching dark matter. The creator drew Tiernon's soul through the dark matter and he entered a new world. The darkness was gone and in its place was a dazzling light.

Tiernon's soul glowed white and took the shape of his earthly body. He walked through a field of tall grass, following a winding path towards a large hill. At the top of the hill were two huge trees on either side of the path. The trees had many branches sprouting from their trunks, which were broad and strong, resembling the Oak. Tiernon knew that this was the Tree of Knowledge and the Tree of Life. He could see a great burning fire that was flickering at the foot of the Tree of Knowledge. The fire glowed with a power of its own and Tiernon could not bear to keep his eyes on it, so he stared transfixed to the floor. The fire burst into a glowing light that blazoned with power and awe.

Tiernon's heart was elated, yet heavy and tears welled in his eyes. He knew that he was in the presence of something great although he was unsure of what it was.

A solemn voice rose from within the flames, "I am the creator of the earth, wind and stars, of the moon and the sun, of your father Taranis and all the Gods you serve. Through my power the universe was born. I set the wheels of the world in motion. I am the ruler of all."

Tiernon was transfixed and stared on as the voice from the holy flame continued.

"You are the first of your kind to see me and it is important that you understand what I am about to tell you."

Tiernon had many questions to ask but was unable to speak, unable to move and unable to unlock his gaze, which was transfixed towards the ground as the voice from within the flames continued, "The quest to save your people depends upon the safe return of the stone. But I tell you now that this is no ordinary stone. This is a seed from the Tree of Immortality."

Tiernan's eyes stared in awe as the creator spoke on. "Your reward for this deed will be a parchment that will lead you to the land of safe haven where the twins will establish a new kingdom. I tell you now that this reward is for the chosen ones and the people of the Celtic line. Your destiny, however and the destiny of the druid lineage will be very different."

The voice of the creator paused for a moment as if choosing the right words to say and the flame shone brighter as the voice spoke on, "The plight of all druids at the hands of the invaders from overseas will be of total annihilation. I tell you the truth."

Tiernon gazed petrified at the ground, great tears welled in his eyes and he swallowed a large lump that had risen in his throat. Still transfixed by some ancient power, he was unable to utter a single sound and was forced to listen in pain as the voice from the flames spoke on, "Shylah has the sight of prophecy but she cannot always see the way. The seed has significance beyond imagination, for the seed is from my Tree of Life. I hold the power to use it but the Evil One also has the power to nurture this seed; to plant this seed on earth and inflict irreparable damage. Anyone who eats the fruit from this tree will become immortal. The Evil One will use this to make every spawn and beast within his power immortal, creating a great and powerful army that will engulf all mankind."

The creator paused for a moment in thought and then continued. "The seed was lost for an age until by chance it turned up in the possession of the brave Bucca, who are now in danger of losing the seed to the Evil One. Although I have told you that the druid line will be lost to the invaders from overseas, I tell you now that I created your kind and all humanity. Trust in me and do my bidding and at the end of ages I will restore your people."

The Creator saw that Tiernon's faith was growing stronger as he said to him, "You shall be my disciple, the one that will not appear in the written word but the one I shall remember, come Judgement Day. Believe in me and you will possess in your palms not only the power of your Father Taranis, but the wrath and fury of the creator."

The creator paused a moment longer before continuing. "Now I order you to return to your body and finish your search. Make your choice to save the seed of immortality, for it will lead to the salvation of the Celtic line in this life and your salvation in the next life. Do not tell the others what you have witnessed. They would not understand and the quest will fail"

The Creators flames soared high into the air and shone brighter as they rose until they disappeared in a blast of thick smoke. Within the blink of an eye Tiernon was thrust back through the darkness of the universe and returned to his limp body.

*

Breanna was on night watch. The rest of the group were sound asleep except for Delano, who was shuffling back and forth, restless and ever listening for danger. Breanna heard a noise come from Tiernon that unnerved her. It was as though Tiernon had risen from the depths of a river after lying at the bottom until almost dead; scrambling to the surface just in time to take a huge breath. His eyes opened wildly as he struggled for air. Finally, after a few panic-stricken moments, he began breathing normally and the colour returned to his cheeks. He sat bolt upright and began taking in his surroundings. This proved difficult for the night was dark and the moon rested behind heavy clouds.

Delano rushed to the side of his old friend. Something was very different about Tiernon. Delano helped him to his feet and walked him around to try to get some circulation running back into his body. It was then that a small thread of light seeped into the camp through a break in the clouds. Delano got a good look at Tiernon and realised with astonishment that his hair and beard were pure white and shimmering like silk. He looked visibly older and many times wiser. Delano enquired with awe, "What has happened to you? You have been near death for many days. I feared for your life and now that you are awake and your hair is pure white."

Tiernon remembered his strange encounter. He knew that it was not a dream and remembered his promise to keep quiet. He answered sternly, "I have been to the end of the Universe and back again. I know my place in this life and you must trust me and follow me, but please do not speak another word about it for I am forbidden to answer you."

Delano replied in earnest, "I understand. I have something for you; I hope it will lift your spirits?"

He then handed over Tiernon's beloved banner of the White Bear talisman, and it did the trick. Tiernon thanked him graciously and put it in his robe for safekeeping.

Chapter 9

The Grindylow

The next morning the group reunited over breakfast happy to see each other safe. The twins stared continuously at Tiernon's new hair colour, but they dare not say a word as Delano warned them not to question him.

Vaughan had been fishing in a lake that he had discovered not too far away. He caught some trout which he had been smoking over the fire for a good while. They tasted good, especially to Tiernon, who knew that he had witnessed death but feared death no more.

*

After their hearty breakfast the group gathered all they could carry and set off on foot towards the vast open marshes and swamps, dumping their cart as it was useless in this landscape. The land was covered by water and it was difficult for them to see where the water ended and where the land began. They trod carefully along small strips of dry land but the further they went the wetter the land became. It was a long journey through this wasteland and the sun was creeping high into the sky.

Delano spoke in earnest to the group, "Be careful. From here on the water has saturated the land so much that the land is like the water itself."

He took the lead and transformed into the wolf. With his keen sense of smell he made his way safely through the mire and the group followed in his tracks, trying their best not to step even the slightest inch out of them.

*

On they travelled well into the day with the sun scorching upon their backs. Breanna had become extremely weary, to the point where she began to lose her concentration. She dropped to the back of the group and began to stumble from the safe path unnoticed by the others, for they had their own burdens to bear.

On and on trudged the weary group and Breanna dropped further away from the rest. She tried desperately to keep up, but hunger was calling and the heat from the sun had exhausted all her strength. Kael was the first to notice that Breanna was no longer with them. He turned around to look for her and was surprised that she had fallen so far behind. He informed the rest of the group and they quickly retraced their steps with caution towards her.

Breanna was now feeling desperately thirsty and she stood motionless, staring into a patch of clear water that was free from the algae and marsh plants. She must surely have been hallucinating for she thought that she could see two piercing eyes staring back at her from beneath the water. They gripped her attention and drew her closer to the water's edge. She leaned forward to take a better look, ignoring the calls of her friends urging her to step back. Then very swiftly a large creature lept from the depths and grabbed Breanna with two strong hands, somersaulting in mid-air and returning to the water in one foul swoop.

Kael was almost upon her at that instant and he got a clear view of the nasty beast. It had the head and torso of a dragon-like creature, with dark green hair running down its back. It had rounded shoulders and huge muscular arms and clawed crooked hands. From the waist down it resembled a large slimy eel with a long thick tail that was heavily armoured with thick scales.

The creature was the Grindylow, an ancient beast of the marshes, sent by the Evil One to capture the children. Kael drew his short sword as he dived into the water and gave chase to the monster which had unnaturally great speed and grace. He struggled to keep up but swam as fast as his arms would take him. The water was murky for the algae grew in abundance making visibility almost impossible. It was not long before Kael needed a breath and he returned to the surface for air. He could see Tiernon standing at the side of the water and he spluttered to him, "Do something. The creature is too fast, I cannot keep up!"

Unfortunately Tiernon still felt weakened by his ordeal and was unable to assist. Delano was already in the water. He had taken the shape of the huge black bear and he searched frantically under the marsh. He too found it hard going and had to return to the surface for air. Vaughan shouted from the patch of dry land, "Look out, the creature is returning."

The Grindylow came back swiftly. Breanna was gone and the creature grabbed Kael firmly in both hands. Kael slashed at him wildly with his sword, but the Grindylow was so huge and his skin was so tough that the cuts were like small scratches. Delano had the chance to pounce onto the back of the creature and he clung on with all his might as the creature swam deeper. Meanwhile Tiernon summoned his sister, Shylah, but this time he used a different chant from the ones that he had used before. This time he asked her to bring her battle ox, a gift from the Gods that had fought bravely in battle against the evil Knuckers, or swamp dragons as they were commonly called in the ancient days. The battle ox was a large creature, bull like in appearance, with large horns and a massive and well rounded muscular body. It had the ability to glide through the water with the speed of a charging pony and rather than swim, it galloped effortlessly through the murky abyss.

*

The Grindylow swam swiftly on until it eventually reached a large cave that grew out from underneath the water, where he deposited Kael, who was exhausted, on to dry land next to the listless body of Breanna. He lay there helpless on the ground with his sword still in his hand, panting for air. Delano was still clinging on to the Grindylow's back and as it returned to the water he was forced to loosen his tight grip, for he too was desperate to breathe. He swam for the entrance of the underwater cave to catch a breath of air, but swiftly and without mercy the Grindylow was upon him clutching him by the waist, dragging him back under the water. Delano punched him several times in the face with his massive bear paws, drawing blood from his nose, but still the Grindylow maintained his strong grip and kept swimming deeper still to drown poor Delano. The water about them suddenly began to boil as huge bubbles erupted from all around and the ground shook like an earthquake. The Grindylow swam in circles searching on all sides to see what was making the rumbling.

From the murk the huge battle ox approached with ease and grace as if running through the water. Shylah was astride the great shoulders of the beast upon a leather saddle. She steered the ox skilfully through the water with the aid of two leather straps that were attached to a huge gold ring through the ox's nose. Shylah was wearing a short shimmering dress made from fine chain mail and leather trousers.

She held in her hand a long sword that shone like a beacon. This was an ancient sword with magical strength, fashioned from steel that was not of this world. The Gods presented it to Shylah for the use in ancient battles between good and evil.

*

The Grindylow had a look of terror on his face. Once he realised what was upon him he let loose his grip on Delano, enabling the Pooka to swim to the safety of the cave. The Grindylow held still in the water with his strong arms outstretched as the huge ox drew closer. He grasped it by the horns with both hands and attempted to halt the ox's progress.

Although they were evenly matched in size, this proved to be a difficult task and the ox maintained its pace, driving the Grindylow backwards in the water. The Grindylow drew on every ounce of strength, twisting the ox's head from side to side to break its neck, but the bullock was strong and soldiered on. Eventually the ox pierced the creature clean in the chest. With a huge roar of pain the Grindylow let loose his firm grip, but sprang swiftly forward and grasped the ox in a deadly headlock. He squeezed with all his might and the ox slowed its pace until halting in the water, choking for air with its life swiftly ebbing away. For a moment the battle looked as if it was surely lost but the ox had a secret weapon. It mustered up all the breath it could and shot huge jets of hot steam from its nostrils, which made the water around it bubble. The Grindylow squealed in agony as the hot blast burned his body. He loosened his grip and received yet another agonising blow to the body from the ox's huge horn, which caught him through the torso impaling him to the face of the ox and unable to free himself. Shylah stood up in her saddle with sword in one hand and the leather straps in the other. While the Grindylow struggled frantically to break free Shylah swung the sword around her head to gain momentum and with one swipe of the magical sword she separated the beast's head from its body. The head sank like a huge boulder to the murky depths as the body twitched until it hung still and lifeless. The ox lowered its head and shook it from side to side until the Grindylow's body slipped off the horn and sank to the depths. The battle was over, but Shylah searched frantically for the trio whom the creature had stolen. The ox had good senses and followed a trail straight to the underwater cave where the trio was recovering from their ordeal. Kael was astounded to see the great Shylah approaching from the depths dressed for battle and riding such a grand beast.

The ox lifted its head slightly out of the water revealing Shylah to the group and she spoke to them, "The danger has passed for

I have destroyed the beast. If you have recovered enough, climb aboard and I will return you to dry land."

Kael stared in bewilderment as he questioned hastily, "Shylah, I never knew that you had such a beast and where did you get such a magnificent sword? Look how it glows."

Shylah smiled as she answered, "There is a great deal that you do not know about me and even more than you need to. As for this great sword. It is called Excalibur and I am its guardian. Never has it failed me for it has magical powers."

Breanna could not contain her excitement as she threw in a question of her own.

"Look at the scabbard, it is decorated with such beauty."

Shylah looked down at the scabbard, still in awe of its majesty despite the many years that she had owned it as she replied, "The scabbard has a special power of its own. The person who has the scabbard in their possession will not show any wound, will lose no blood and will not fail in any battlefield against any foe. The sword and scabbard were a gift from the Gods, full of great magic, wisdom and power. I am the keeper of the sword and it is my duty to hide the sword in a secret place, away from any mortal and any beast. I only use the sword when nothing else will prevail. Enough questions, I must get you back with the others."

The trio climbed onto the back of the ox. Delano transformed into his Pooka form for he found it easier to ride the beast that way. They all took deep breaths as the ox sank under the water but it did not take long for the ox to return them to dry land.

Tiernon and Vaughan were delighted to see their friends safe again and they all embraced each other joyously.

Shylah rose from the water on her majestic beast. She noticed the change in Tiernon straight away but simply acknowledged him with a nod of her head. The ox was sniffing at Tiernon like an excited puppy, for he was a very old friend. Tiernon rubbed its huge face lovingly with both hands and patted it rewardingly several times. The ox loved the attention and with a swipe of its huge tongue, it licked Tiernon right across his face leaving a trail of thick slime.

Breanna took one look at him as if she was about to vomit and said, "That looks really bad."

Tiernon's smile left him and he was trying his best to hide his displeasure whilst he was spitting out the residue from his mouth. It was a funny moment and the group found themselves laughing aloud.

Shylah was the first to resume her concentration as she spoke to Tiernon, "I must return the sword to its rightful place. I will give you the use of my ox. It will offer you protection and take you quickly through this watery wasteland to the forest further southwards, but from there on I fear that you are on your own. Goodbye my brother."

Shylah sank beneath the water and disappeared.

*

The group climbed aboard the giant ox. There was plenty of room but it was an uncomfortable ride, for the saddle was only big enough for one person. Tiernon was the only one who had the skill to ride the beast so he took the best seat. The ox swam high in the water and kept going at a good pace for almost two days until reaching the vast forest. They took turns to pat the beast thankfully on the head and the ox returned to where it had come from. somewhere deep, dark and forgotten.

Chapter 10

The Realm of Elgon

Hunting was good in this part of the forest; it seemed like a friendly place full of kind spirits and beings. Breanna had the chance many times to prove her skill with the bow, bringing a hearty meal back every day. She caught boar, deer, hares and a beaver.

The group travelled by day and camped at night taking turns to keep watch for danger whilst the others slept. Tiernon took this time of relative peacefulness to sharpen Kael's skill with the sword.

Vaughan kept a tidy camp and took care of the cooking. Delano took regular solitary trips to check for danger.

On one of his excursions Delano caught a scent of something familiar in the air. Although it was faint he recognised it from his time spent at the great fort, which seemed like such a long time ago. He sniffed the air many times, taking in the aroma to be sure before making up his mind and then he returned to camp and spoke to Tiernon.

"I can smell burning like that of iron smelting, like the smell that used to come from the blacksmith's hut in the fort. It is unmistakable to me."

Tiernon looked a little bemused as he replied, "Are you sure? I cannot smell it. Where is it coming from?"

Delano pointed the way as he said, "It is coming from the south. It is a faint smell so I believe it is a good few miles away, but I am sure that there must be a settlement there."

Tiernon replied thoughtfully, "We must be in the realm of the Dumnonii Clan. They are the tin people of the Brythonic dialect. I know of their King. He is known as a brave and worthy man."

Vaughan left his cooking pot bubbling whilst he informed Tiernon, "I have kinsmen in this area. They say that the Dumnonii are a friendly sort. They do not deal in coins, so they are free from greed and want."

Tiernon pondered on this for a while longer before making up his mind and then he instructed Delano, "Follow the scent trail to their fort. I think it should be safe. We have spent quite enough time in the forest and the barren lands in our attempt to evade our own kind. I think it will be uplifting to see people that remind us of home."

*

The group agreed that this was a fantastic idea and followed Delano as he picked out the most direct trail, taking care not to lose the scent.

It was in fact a lot further than Delano had first suspected, for the group had to camp down for another two nights before they got close to the settlement. Delano slowed his pace and he glared through the thick forest where he could see that there was an opening not too far away. He gestured to the others with his hands and they peered into that direction but could see nothing as they did not possess the great vision that Delano had. They followed single file through the thick scrub. The tension was rising, along with the excitement of meeting people of their own kind. The forest began to thin out and the group was walking through carpets of bluebells and patches of foxgloves.

At the edge of the forest, Delano shifted into bear form and spoke to the others, "Wait here a moment. I will look to make sure it is safe."

He left the cover of the bushes and ventured into an open field. He knew there was a settlement nearby. He looked out from the undergrowth and spied a large fort about a mile from where he was standing. He returned to his Pooka form and beckoned the others to follow. They emerged into the light and made their way steadily towards the large fort. Tiernon found his beloved banner from within his robe and held it aloft so that the White Bear emblem could be seen blowing in the wind. It was not long before the group was near the fort gates and the lookout was quick to blow his warning horn. He then noticed the banner and was stricken with awe as he shouted. "The mighty Tiernon and the chosen are approaching. Welcome Tiernon, we have awaited your coming."

Tiernon was pleased to find a friendly face but a little dismayed that The Dumnonii already knew that they were coming. This meant that word had travelled quickly and the evil forces would certainly know their whereabouts too.

The gates opened and the group introduced themselves to the Dumnonii nobility and their king, Maccus, meaning the hammer. He was a brave and noble warrior in battle whose weapon of choice was a double-sided club hammer mounted on a long slender pole of hickory, originally used for crushing rocks into small pieces to gain access to their tin content. The group followed the King to the largest hut at the centre of the fort, which Kael and Breanna recognised as the hut of the nobility. They sat around the fire and spoke of their journey, making plans for the impending search of the swamp dragon. King Maccus was the first to speak.

"You have travelled far to get to this part of the country. I surmise that you have met with foul creatures, but I must warn you, the swamp dragon is as cunning as a fox, strong as an ox and clever like the wolf."

Delano leant forward to respond, "I too am all those things and I speak for all of us when I say that the swamp dragon is no match for us."

Tiernon raised his hand in defiance and sharply jumped in with a comment of his own.

"My old friend, please do not underestimate the might of Elgon, the swamp dragon. It is no coincidence that he is still alive after years of plunder."

King Maccus spoke sternly towards the group. "Our village came under threat many years ago, when the waste from our tin manufacturing found its way into the river that runs down to the coast and into Elgon's cave, killing the fish that he fed upon. Hunger caused him to venture up river to our camp. The swamp dragon would feed on our livestock and any human who was foolish enough to swim in the river. Elgon forced us to dig large pits to catch the green waste before it entered the river. He made us pour the waste on the hillside and plant upon it heather and gorse. We cleaned up our tin processes thinking that this would appease Elgon, but he relished in our fear and has cursed us ever since. We have paid handsomely for dragon slayers and they have all failed to kill the beast."

*

Breanna was keen to have her say, "My bow fires the swiftest and straightest of arrows. I will pierce the dragon's heart with my arrow and bring down the beast."

Troubled by his sister's remarks, Kael scorned her. "What makes you think that your arrow will kill the beast? My sword will pierce his heart."

The king admired the children for their brave words but could not help the anxious gaze that he gave to them as he responded, "The swamp dragon has skin as hard as granite, claws like large iron daggers and teeth as long as your sword. His body is large with a well-rounded torso. He has a huge head with a bony plate that protrudes around his shoulders. He has a powerful bite that can crush a man's skull as if it was made of chalk. Bony growths run down his back; anyone who touches these spines is shredded and cut. Do not be fooled by his short legs; they are thick set and very powerful. He is surprisingly swift and agile both in water and on land."

Vaughan sat quietly for a moment in deep thought before questioning. "Does anyone know if the dragon has a weakness?"

The King replied in earnest, "He has no weakness. He is remarkably fast on land in short bursts. He can scale sheer cliffs using his massive claws for grip. His tail is also a handy weapon and he can decapitate a man with one blow."

Vaughan looked frantically for someone to offer any reassurance, but none was forthcoming.

The King spoke on, "We have to make a human sacrifice to the beast every year, as a token of respect, to appease the swamp dragon and keep him from plundering the whole village. Your arrival to our land is a blessing. If you destroy this beast then our lives will be changed forever."

Tiernon looked down at the ground. His mind was a swirl with his own questions regarding his intentions should he succeed in slaying the dragon and the choices he would make concerning the seed of the Tree of Immortality. Keeping his thoughts to himself he said nothing of it and the discussion went on well into the long hours.

*

The next morning King Maccus met the group in the blacksmith's quarters and kitted them out in protective chain mail and headgear. Vaughan even managed to find the correct size for his small frame. Delano and Tiernon declined the offer, choosing to go to battle as they had done many times before with only their wits for protection. The gates opened and the group left the fort in the direction of the coastline. Kael looked to his left and noticed the hillside covered in green-purple and yellow plantation. He had never seen such a rugged landscape with its man-made hills and crags and was in awe of the vast number of insects that fluttered about on fragile wings. A huge buzzard soared high in the sky, searching for small mammalian morsels that scampered about the rocks for protection. He watched it stop and hover lightly in one spot for a second before swooping down out of sight for a few moments and reappearing with a shrew in its talons.

*

The group arrived at the river that flowed all the way to the coastal cliffs and followed this for many miles. King Maccus halted the group with a hand gesture and spoke quietly. "We are getting closer to the dragon's lair."

He pointed to a large hole in the ground as he informed the group, "That hole opens out into Elgon's cave. If we go that way, he will surely see us. We must circle quietly around it and climb down the cliffside to the seashore. There is an entrance through a small cave from below, but we must be silent in our descent."

The group walked around the large hole keeping well away from the edge so as not to cast any giveaway shadow into the murky blackness below.

The landscape here was different. The ground was hilly and sandy with short, green grass growing weakly all around, with scattered pink, purple and yellow flowers delicately swaying in the breeze. In places taller grass grew in abundance on the sand dunes; this was different from any grass that grew in Brigantes. It was flat at the base and pointed at the ends with long slender spikes which stabbed at the skin like the bite of a small snake. The group reached the cliff's edge. Kael and Breanna stopped dead in their tracks as they got their first ever glimpse of the mighty sea. Their view spanned for miles around. In the distance stood two small islands, lonely rocks that had once been connected to the land but had given way to the sea millions of years before. The sea disappeared into the distant horizon and Kael spoke in wonder, "I can see the end of the earth."

Tiernon laughed loudly because like all well informed Druids, he knew that the earth was round.

The climb down to the shore was a difficult and dangerous one. The granite stone was sharp and cut the delicate hands of the children, but they plodded on bravely and never once cried out in pain. Vaughan was the best climber out of the group, trotting down the cliff face nimbly and light of foot, making almost no noise at all. He was closest to the bottom when he noticed the rocks becoming a little slimy under foot. There were many nooks and crannies about him filled with seawater where green seaweed grew in abundance. He paused for a moment to inspect one closer and was surprised by the number of small fish that were swimming about and purple blobs clinging to the rock. A crab took cover under the green seaweed as his shadow blocked out the sun and a small fish darted swiftly for cover. Vaughan mused to himself; he liked this new world.

He gestured to the children as they approached, "Come and look at this, it is truly amazing."

The children almost forgot their task once they spied the world of the rock pools. They scampered eagerly from pool to pool in anticipation as they searched for more small creatures.

Delano scoffed quietly yet abruptly, "Kael, Breanna, stop that at once! We have to be watchful of danger."

Although these were battle hardy and well-trained children, they were children all the same and began sulking at the prospect of a good roasting.

*

The group of warriors gathered on the sand at the foot of the cliff. The sun was bright and the sea was a good distance away. The waves were thrashing at the sand as the sea was slowly approaching the cliffs and white froth leapt high and fast like white stallions leaping fences. King Maccus gestured to the group to follow and he lead them past many caves that were scattered along the coastline before settling upon an entrance that encroached about twenty feet into the cliff side, becoming narrower until it ended in a sharp point.

Tiernon investigated the cave and asked sternly, "Is this the correct entrance? It does not go anywhere."

King Maccus looked upwards and the group stared up to see that the cave roof opened out into a huge archway. They could see three separate rounded chambers that led in different directions and were roughly six feet in diameter, just large enough for a man to crawl through.

King Maccus lectured the group. "Each hole ventures deep into the cliff for just over a mile. They veer in all directions but eventually meet up at the centre of the cliff depths and into Elgon's lair. I think that we should split into three groups, that way we will tread lightly. We can hide in the holes near the lair until we are all ready to move in."

Tiernon was quick to step in. "Do not make a move until we are all safely in place."

Delano glanced towards Tiernon as he asked, "How will we know when we are all ready in the darkness?"

King Maccus answered, "The hole that we passed at the top of the cliff leads directly into the dragon's cave. It lets enough light through for us to see each other. That is why we could not enter that way, Elgon would have seen us straight away."

The group clambered steadily up the side walls of the cave. The climb was not that hard, the rocks were big enough to get a good firm hand hold and easy enough to find good footing. As the group got closer to each hole, they split up. Delano and Kael took the left entrance. Tiernon and Vaughan took the middle entrance and King Maccus and Breanna took the entrance to the right. As the warriors clambered further into the chambers they became a little narrower and the light behind them slowly faded. The holes were surprisingly smooth and became even smoother as the group progressed. They could have been forgiven for thinking that the chambers were natural occurrences created thousands of years earlier by the sea.

They were in fact created by the Knockers, or Bucca as they were known in this part of the world. The Bucca were small people with well-rounded shoulders and muscular forearms, formed through years of labour and toil. They were like dwarfs but did not have bearded faces and were always clean-shaven men. The difference between a Bucca and a dwarf, apart from the lack of facial hair, was their ability to knock on hard stone with their tough hand and with their ears to the ground, listening intently to the sound which they used to interpret whether there was anything precious in the ground. The well-attuned Bucca could even identify what was there simply by the sound of the knock. The older Bucca would grow huge bumps on the knuckle joints between their fingers from the years of constant knocking; that is how they got their name. The word Bucca was from the Brythonic language but had the same meaning. The Bucca had found precious stones within the cave many years before. They had mined the three chambers deep within the cliff in their constant search for precious stones and the main shaft that led downwards from the cliff top was their air shaft. Elgon had climbed down the shaft many years ago and discovered the Bucca. He devoured them one by one, forcing them to hide deeper and deeper in smaller crevices under the earth. Anyone brave enough to venture out would be eaten. The Bucca pulled together and a great battle had ensued between the brave little mining people and Elgon. Unfortunately, they were overthrown by the beast and their land was stolen, but that is another story.

*

The warriors continued, oblivious to the sad past that lay within the chambers. The light had all but disappeared and the group trundled blindly in the darkness on hands and knees. All were developing nasty red patches on their knees because of the constant crawling; only Delano escaped the pain for he had his thick fur for protection. However, because he was the largest of the group, he struggled to squeeze through the tight spaces.

Tiernon had a good guide in Vaughan.

The tunnels went on and on, up and down, east to west; in differing directions, which confused the travellers.

Tiernon and Vaughan could hear the drips of water falling from above. As they ventured on the drips became louder. Tiernon realised that they were approaching the entrance to Elgon's lair. He tugged on Vaughan's shorts, then indicated with a finger to his lips that they needed to be very quiet.

A dim light shone into the tunnel in front of them. It was not long before the hole became wider and easier to navigate and the duo eventually reached an open platform that they could both sit on. Vaughan peered down into the cave below. It opened out into a vast chasm. A shaft of light broke the darkness from a gaping hole in the roof of the cave. Vaughan traced the light from the top to the bottom. He noticed a large lake below fed by a stream of fresh water that seemed to appear through solid rock. This was ground water that had travelled many miles from faraway places, bringing with it rich sediment. The rock from where it came was covered in a strange, shiny green pigment, giving the rock a slippery appearance. With his keen eyes Vaughan spied into every nook and cranny from his vantage point. He could see large rocks scattered about the ground in messy piles which had fallen from the ceiling due to the constant mining of the Bucca, leaving behind beautifully, architectural archways.

Tiernon tapped Vaughan gently on the shoulder as he asked, "Can you see any sign of Elgon?"

Vaughan replied softly, "He is not here. I can see almost every crevice and all the rocks below and he is not among them."

At that moment some movement from across the cave caught Vaughan's eye. It was Breanna and King Maccus. They scrambled from their hole on to a platform and waved across at Tiernon and Vaughan, who were quite visible as the light shaft gave away their silhouette. The group then sat in quietness and waited for Delano and Kael, who were not doing very well at all, for Delano had become wedged tight. Kael was pushing with all his might but the hole seemed to shrink around the Pooka.

Delano managed to gasp. "It is no good. The deeper I go the smaller it gets. I am going to have to go backwards and make my way back to the cliff top."

Kael struggled to budge the Pooka and responded with a groan, "You cannot do that. It would take you too long and we need you in the cave. I will give you a push. Try stretching your arms out in front while I push your feet."

Delano responded sharply, "If I go any further I won't be able to move at all. I can only go back. It is the only way."

Just then a small voice from an unseen place broke in, "It is not the only way my good warrior. I will show you another way."

Kael turned around swiftly as the small voice was coming from directly behind him. He stared intently but could see nothing at all as the voice spoke again.

"Is it true? Am I correct in assuming that you have come to slay the Dragon and free our people?"

Delano could only lie there quite helpless. He attempted to turn his head to get a glimpse of the fellow that was speaking, but it was no good. Kael put a hand in front and felt about for a person, but none was forthcoming.

Kael replied, "If it pleases you, we will destroy the Dragon and free your people. Come on now, show yourself."

Suddenly a hole appeared from within the rock, as a stone circle seemed to roll itself left to right, to reveal a much larger circular opening. Light trickled in from the new aperture and there stood a Bucca. Kael, who had never in his entire life seen or heard of such a person, just stared with wonder.

The Bucca broke the awkward silence and spoke again. "Quick, get in here. I will free your friend. It is a bit wider down here."

Kael was quick to trust the little, strange person and retreated into the hole. To his amazement it opened out into a wide tunnel with smooth sided walls, littered with a row of burning torches fastened to iron baskets. Kael could see that the walls were high and there was a staircase beneath his feet. The Bucca then crawled out into the space that Kael had retreated from and he grasped Delano firmly around his ankles as he said, "Are you ready? I am going to pull you back so that you can free yourself."

Kael cackled and said rudely, "How do you expect to free the mighty Delano? You are smaller than me and I could not budge him."

Kael almost swallowed his words for the Bucca popped Delano from his position like a cork from a bottle as if he weighed nothing at all.

Delano scrambled quickly into the larger tunnel to join Kael and the kind Bucca that had helped him was quick to follow. He grasped Kael firmly by the shoulder with one hand and tensed his massive bicep of his free arm as he said, "In answer to your question my little fellow, look at that. Small I may be but strong in stature am I. Please do not insult me again."

Kael could not help but gasp. The Bucca's arm was truly massive in comparison to his small size, not to mention his forearm and shoulder. The Bucca explained, "These muscles do not grow on trees. They are shaped through many years of toil, lifting rocks and digging. We may be small but we are mighty. We must move onwards, we have no time. Elgon awaits you hidden among the rocks."

Delano and Kael followed the Bucca down the stairs and deep into the earth, wondering intently where this journey would lead them.

*

Tiernon was growing anxious. He was sure that there was no danger from Elgon as it appeared that the chasm below was devoid of life. Tiernon spoke out aloud.

"Delano, where are you?"

His voice resonated through the cave and loudly echoed three times. An evil voice replied.

"Sons of Celtus, warriors from Gaul,
Come to my house and try to take all.
On the Quest for a land of the free.
You have no chance. You must get by me."

Tiernon and the group all stared in the direction of the evil voice, but all they could see were rocks.

93

The voice spoke again.

"Tiernon of the troubled mind.
This God or that God, your faith is blind.
Should ye continue or should ye not.
Take the seed and lose the lot.
Your faith in the moon, the stars and the sun.
Tested this day will you stay, or run?
Leave the seed within my care,
I will let you live and your life I will spare.
Live a long life in religion of old.
Out with the new, grow wise and grow bold.
Leave now and be spared and go free,
Never to face attack from the men from the sea"

*

Tiernon felt unnerved by the knowledge of the unseen beast. To the others in his company the beast spoke in a riddle but Tiernon understood every word. Tiernon was angered and spoke sternly but not aloud; he spoke directly to the dragon using the power of his mind.

"Do not waste my time with riddles and empty words for I have seen the truth with my own eyes. I have seen the Creator and he has shown me the way. My task shall be done and I will fight you this day."

The Dragon gave a low cackle as he replied. "You are a fool. Even with the knowledge that your people will perish, you are still prepared to retrieve the seed. You old and foolish Druid"

Suddenly the Dragon stopped speaking as Tiernon interrupted loudly using his powers of telepathy. "Be silent you beast of lies. I am commanded by one more powerful than you. I will receive my reward at the end of ages. I will no longer bandy words with an evil swamp coward of the darkness. Show yourself and prepare to die."

Tiernon scampered swiftly down the chasm walls taking no time searching for his footing. It seemed to come naturally. He had all but forgotten the others, who realised that he was heading to battle and followed him as quickly as they dare.

Tiernon was the first to the ground and he rushed to the rocks to where the voice was coming from. He spoke bravely, "Show yourself and prepare for your end. I am the mighty Tiernon."

To his astonishment, the large rock in front of him began to shake, revealing a tail and then a leg and then a face and a pair of eyes until the complete beast had metamorphosed from the stone. It paced up and down violently before stooping its head low to the ground with its face right up to the nose of Tiernon, then it spoke menacingly yet quietly, "No, it is not my turn to die this day for it appears who you have made your choices so you are the one who will die."

Tiernon quickly pointed out both arms as he shouted, "I give you the wrath of my father Teranis."

Two massive bolts of lightning projected from his hands towards the face of Elgon, lighting up the chasm and casting long sinister shadows. As soon as the blast contacted the swamp dragon, Elgon stooped his head low to the ground and the lightning bolts reflected off the heavy, spiny plate that protected its neck. Tiernon put more and more of his life's energy into the thunderbolts but repeatedly the thick skin of the dragon just cast them aside. Tiernon was so angered that he battled on, firing a continuous stream of lightning into the dragon with new found strength and vigour. Elgon groaned loudly as the pain became unbearable. At last, Tiernon was forcing the dragon back and he was edging forward, growing more and more confident until suddenly and painfully with all his energy spent, Tiernon fell to the ground exhausted. Elgon stood almost motionless for a second or two and then shook his huge head. The other warriors had just managed to scramble to the ground to face Elgon before he fully recovered.

Tiernon lay lifeless and King Maccus was the second brave to enter the fracas. He wielded his mighty hammer and struck it hard on the back of the swamp dragon. On rock the hammer never gave sway, but Elgon was much harder than any rock and the hammer shattered into many small pieces. The pain that shot through the arms of King Maccus was excruciating and he fell to his knees, holding his arms and screaming as if all his bones were broken. Breanna was next to try her luck. She drew her bow several times, but the arrows bounced from the dragon's body by the dozen. Faster and faster she drew each bow but to no avail. Elgon grew tired of this game and edged closer to Breanna for the kill. Vaughan found the strength to pick up a large boulder and hurtled it at Elgon. It bounced off his nose and on to the ground but took with it a large chunk of flesh and at last Elgon showed a sign of weakness as blood flowed freely from the wound. Elgon slashed at Vaughan with one blow, hurtling him across the ground and into unconsciousness, saved from death by the heavy chain mail that was provided by King Maccus. Elgon continued to pursue Breanna. He could finish the others later. Breanna backed off as far as she could until she was cornered. She made a brief attempt to attack the dragon with her dagger but it just ricocheted from his flesh like a sword on stone.

Elgon lifted his mighty foot in the air and paused a moment. "I never thought it would be this easy to destroy the chosen."

From the cave wall an opening appeared from behind Breanna and a pair of small but very muscular hands pulled her inside. Delano then sprang out in his bear form and replied quickly as he caught the dragon's foot in both hands.

"It is not going to be that easy for you Elgon. I am Delano and I will kill you with my bare hands."

Delano mustered all the strength he could, lifting Elgon's front end clean into the air and with one almighty burst of effort he tipped the dragon on to its back. Without a thought Delano leapt on to the dragon's belly and bludgeoned the dragon with many hard punches to the face. Unfortunately, Delano had forgotten the description of the beast that King Maccus had given days before. He soon realised that the dragon had skin as hard as granite for with each punch came a sickening pain that shot through his arms. He was hurting himself more than he was hurting Elgon.

Kael was watching from within the opening, and he noticed that Delano was weakening. Elgon swung his tail wildly and caught Delano on the side of the face, knocking him into the air and on to the hard floor. Kael, with no thought for his own safety sprang into action leaping on to Elgon's belly with his sword at the ready. He lifted the sword above his head for a moment before slashing hard on to Elgon's belly. He was sure to kill the swamp dragon, but the sword simply ricocheted as it struck the dragon's hard exterior. Elgon grabbed Kael in one massive-clawed hand as he returned swiftly to all fours. He squeezed Kael hard and pinned him forcefully to the ground. Breanna tried desperately to help her brother but the Bucca held on to her and would not let her go. It was futile to let her risk her life.

It was over. The cause was lost.

Tiernon lay lifeless on the ground a few feet away. His eyes closed and his mind fell into darkness. A voice entered his head that he recognised. It was the voice of the Creator.

"You have shown your faith in me when you chose to give your life and remain true to the quest for the seed. You took heed of what I told you and still you risked your life to save it. I give you back your life as reward. Now get up, Tiernon and use your bolts of lightning again, but this time do not use the wrath of your father. Instead, use the wrath of The Creator. Get up. I command you. Get up."

Tiernon leapt from the ground like a dog to a bone, pointing his hands towards the Dragon.

Elgon slowly approached Tiernon as if stalking him. He had a grin on his now scarred face as he watched Tiernon, waiting for him to fire his futile bolts of lightning.

Tiernon spoke sternly and solemnly with strength in his voice. "By the wrath of the Creator, give me your strength."

As the last word left Tiernon's lips, Elgon's smile turned to dismay as he had no time to react. Two massive bolts of lightning struck Elgon with all the power of the universe. With a loud scream the dragon endured the pain as the energy surged through his body, burning into his muscles and fibres and every nerve ending. Elgon held his head low as he tried to protect himself with his neck shield. He screamed loudly as his face grimaced with pain, which he fought as he edged slowly towards Tiernon until he could take no more. His hard skin glowed orange and yellow until turning white hot like iron in a furnace, and he exploded into a thousand pieces as rocky flesh bounced from every wall. Blood gushed out on to the ground, running into the lake, turning it a deep sombre red.

Elgon would no longer plunder the village of the Dumnonii, nor would he squat in the home of the Bucca. Elgon was gone. Elgon the swamp dragon was dead.

Chapter 11

The Men-an-Tol

A strange and rhythmical chanting rumbled from within the walls as many voices could be heard singing. "Tiernon the mighty, Tiernon the great. Tiernon the mighty has sealed our fate."

The song continued as circular stone doors were rolled open and large crowds of Bucca began to stream out from their hiding places into the open chasm. The leader still had a firm hold on Breanna but once he realised it was safe, he let her go. She kicked him hard in the shin and ran to the side of her brother, who lay helpless on the floor. As Tiernon looked about he saw that Delano was sprawled out unconscious whilst Vaughan was strewn across a rock where he fell in the fracas. King Maccus was knelt in wretched pain, still holding his arms that were clearly broken into painful pieces.

As Tiernon stared failure in the face he was surrounded by many small and stout yet powerful men and women, all cheering for him, edging closer until the leader spoke. "Tiernon the mighty, you have freed our people from a prison which we have endured generation after generation for over two hundred years. How can we ever repay you?"

Tiernon pushed past the worshipping crowd in search of Breanna, who held her brother in her arms and sobbed loudly, "He is dying Tiernon. Elgon has crushed the very life out of him. He is barely breathing."

Tiernon inspected Kael closely to see the chain mail armour crushed about his body. His breathing was shallow and weary and his eyes rolled around in his head.

Tiernon took one harsh look at the Bucca leader and said quietly, "If you want to repay me then help the boy and save my friends. If you cannot do such a thing, go away and do not waste my time."

The head Bucca replied in earnest, "We do not have the power to heal but if it pleases you, we can show you how to get to the Men-an-toll, the healing stone."

Tiernon looked in puzzlement as he answered, almost questioned, "The Men-an-Tol!"

*

The Men-an-Tol was an ancient stone at least two days travel southwards towards the Land's End. The Men-an-Tol was laid two thousand years before the Celts arrived by the first wave of early man who had come to this land across the great ice barrier. Guided by their faith they used this strange stone to heal the sick. The Celts in the area knew of the stones but only the Bucca, who had been around for much longer, knew about their healing properties.

Tiernon looked gravely towards the Bucca as he pleaded, "Can you take us there? I have four men desperate for treatment."

A voice from the murk replied, "Make that three. I was merely unconscious. The beast has a menacing punch."

Tiernon was happy to see his old friend Delano on his feet and in good humour. This often meant that he was alright. A little sore and bruised, but alright. Tiernon looked towards a dark corner as a little movement caught his eye and he was elated to see Vaughan rise to his feet and brush himself down as he said, "Make that two." He was a little shaken up but was relatively unharmed.

Tiernon was pleased to see his two close comrades up on their feet, but his main concern was for the boy. He questioned the Bucca again, "The boy is close to death. How far is this stone?"

The Bucca gave a thoughtful glance as he replied. "On rough track it is very far, but we can take you through our mine. There is a short cut which leads straight to the stones. It should only take a day if we make haste. We shall make a stretcher and wheel the injured party on our carts."

Tiernon had not forgotten the seed of the Tree of Immortality. He soon realised that the seed was nowhere to be seen so he asked the Bucca another question, "It is said that the swamp dragon was guarding an ancient stone. Do you know of its whereabouts?"

The Bucca answered, luckily "Elgon never got his hands on it, or that would have been the end of everything. Instead he stayed in our land for more than two hundred years, plundering our kind, trying to torture us into giving him the stone. We never relinquished it because we knew of the consequence should it fall into evil hands."

Tiernon thoughtfully questioned again, "So am I right in assuming that you have it?"

The Bucca nodded in agreement, "Yes. We have hidden it safely since it came into our keeping. You will be the next to become its guardian. It will be a relief to hand it over for we have suffered enough persecution protecting it. We will give it to you once we have helped the boy and your team is strong enough and fit enough to bear the burden."

Tiernon replied with gratitude, "You are a good man, what is your name?"

The Bucca smiled, "I am Trahern, and I am pleased to be of your service."

*

The Bucca set to work tending to the weary heroes. They brought in two hefty wooden carts, previously used to move large quantities of earth from the mines and set about making stretchers for the stricken King Maccus and for Kael. It took them no time at all, and they were soon on their way southwards down vast wide chambers, which were hidden by secret stone doorways and stairwells. The chamber walls ran high, almost out of sight, and the arches were smooth and shining. The sheer size of the man-made caverns gave insight into the length of time that the Bucca had lived here mining for gold, silver and precious stones. The caverns went on for many miles. It must have taken many years, at least a thousand if not more. The Bucca was indeed an ancient race.

Kael was struggling. Every bump that the cart hobbled over was causing him immense distress and King Maccus did not fare much better. His arms were completely shattered and the pain was sickening, but he was a brave man and barely made a sound.

The Bucca moved swiftly through the many chasms and corridors; sometimes it was hard for Tiernon and his men to keep up with them. The Bucca knew every track and corridor intimately and knew what was around every corner. Although it was hard going keeping pace with them, no one complained because time was of the essence. Kael was dying.

*

They ventured on relentlessly until Tiernon and his men had all but lost track of direction. It sometimes appeared that they had entered the same area twice, but the confidence of the hardy Bucca was reassurance enough that they were going the right way. Outside, the sun was low in the sky and the night was closing in. It would be early morning before the group would get to their goal.

The Bucca switched direction, cutting through an area that looked as if it was undertaking extensive renovation. There were many wooden scaffolds stretching into the abyss tied together with strong rope, rickety and ungainly in appearance. It would take a person with a good head for heights to attempt such monuments. The cave ceiling was propped with long, wooden poles crafted from long, straight, slender trees. A job that would normally have been impossible had it not been for the Bucca's knowledge of pollarding, an ancient art of chopping trees short and forcing them to grow long straight limbs. At the centre of this area of cave sprouted a large man-made column of rock that ran from the floor, towering towards the ceiling.

As Trahern passed this place he turned to the group and said, "We had to renovate this area to save the cliffside from collapse, to prevent Elgon from gaining entrance to our world. We have worked hard keeping Elgon out."

Further on, it was clearly visible to see the many patchwork repairs and stone columns running along an invisible seam of weakness in the land. It was strange to think that any traveller above ground would be oblivious to the danger below.

*

Hunger took its toll and the whole group was beginning to feel the pressure, but Kael was weakening. His breathing had become shallow and his face was ashen. Breanna feared for him and her troubles were written all over her face. It was a relief for everyone that around the next corner shone a small light that grew with every weary step. As the group got closer it became apparent that the light was coming from an opening in the ceiling. The track they were walking on became a little steeper and was difficult to climb. It took three strong Bucca to push each cart towards the opening, to the surprise of Tiernon, who was the first of his troop to venture out. He reached the outside world through a hole in the ground that reminded him of a large badger set. Celts and Druids did not like holes in the ground because of their belief that they led to the underworld. Nobody minded on this occasion because after such a long, tiresome journey in the dark the open air was welcoming. Trahern spoke with great relief,

"Not far to go now, my friends. We have reached the village near the end of the land. The stones are only a few feet away from our secret spot."

Trahern led the group onwards through a field of meadow flowers growing profusely amongst wild grass, which caressed the travellers as they passed by. They ventured purposefully for a while before coming across a great stone monument that was both awe inspiring and strange. It consisted of three large stones that were set out in a triangular formation, seemingly growing naturally from the ground. One stone was leaning over and looked as if it was about to topple, but had in fact stood that way for two thousand years.

A large concentric stone stood alone in the centre amongst its three sisters, which had a hole carved neatly through it. This occupied half its total size and looked big enough for a person to climb through. The early morning sun crept a little higher in the sky, radiating light through the centre stone and casting a strange shadow across the ground, that edged towards the leaning stone.

Trahern looked at Tiernon with a happy smile on his face as he spoke, "This is the Men-an-Tol, the great healing stone. You are blessed that our kind were around to witness its power and therefore have the faith needed for the stone to heal. You are fortunate that the sun is early in the sky, casting a perfect light on to the leaning stone. It is the most powerful time of day to heal the sick."

Tiernon beckoned the bearers of the cart to bring Kael to the stone. Trahern reassured him, "We will take the boy from here."

He ordered his men to place Kael on the leaning stone. Kael was very close to death. The Bucca physically had to hold him against the stone to prevent him from falling over. He had not taken a real breath of clean air for most of the night and his lungs were burning in their attempt to extract every available inch of oxygen. He lay still and lifeless without the will to continue and as the Bucca held him against the stone he gasped his last breath. Tiernon witnessed this moment and rushed forward to reach him, but Trahern grasped him by the forearm with his grip of iron and stopped him short.

"You must not enter the stone circle if you lack just a shred of faith, for it will undermine the power to heal. Do not underestimate our faith in the stones, for we have witnessed many times the power that they yield."

Tiernon was furious and struggled intently to free himself. "Kael is dead you fool. It is too late. We are too late."

Trahern shook his head as he reassured Tiernon, "Trust me my friend. You have shown our people a good turn. Let me do the same for yours. The boy has only just slipped away from us. He can be returned to us."

Tiernon succumbed to the Bucca and let them prepare Kael for his ordeal as he lay lifeless, propped precariously against the leaning stone oblivious to the weeping of his comrades. The Bucca began to chant in a language much older than that of the Celtic tongue. They formed a circle around the stones, linking hands. They proceeded to walk around them. This continued for a short while and the chanting got louder. The sun shone brighter and its radiance flickered on to Kael's lifeless body. Without any instruction the two Bucca that were holding Kael picked him up from his stone and placed him bodily through the centre stone into the hands of two others that were waiting to collect him. The pair then laid him on the grass whilst the group continued to chant.

*

After a short time they placed his body on the leaning stone and repeated the circling until the Bucca once again passed Kael's body through the Men-an-Tol to the waiting pair, who once again laid him on the grass. The process was repeated a third time, passing his body through the Men-an-Tol and laying him on the grass. Kael stayed unresponsive as his friends watched on, powerless. Suddenly, the whole group had a very strange feeling creeping over them, the type of feeling that there was a severe thunderstorm on the horizon. Everything became quiet and the birds stopped singing, the breeze stopped blowing and the weeping ended.

Unable to speak the group looked on as magnetic forces filled the air around them. The sun waned in the sky and the bright blue became overcast with an eerie grey. The clouds rushed by as if pushed by a strong wind but all was silent until a rumble of thunder broke in. Then from nowhere a huge fork of lightning appeared from the sky and shot to the earth with intent towards Kael, striking his body with great speed and accuracy. The sheer force of the bolt lifted his body from the ground and a huge cloud of smoke spilled out from where the lightning had entered his chest. As fast as it appeared it was gone and the grey murky sky gave sway to iridescent blue. The birds began to sing, the sun shone again and Kael woke up, unaware of the events that had just transpired.

Breanna shed tears of joy, as did Tiernon, Delano and Vaughan. Trahern looked at Tiernon with a smile and said cheerfully, "Now you may enter the circle for you have witnessed its power and you now have the faith that the Men-an-Tol is a true wonder of healing."

The group did not need a reminder. They were at Kael's side in an instant and began embracing each other whilst laughing aloud. They had totally forgotten the brave King Maccus waiting patiently for his turn, so he interrupted loudly, "I do not wish to spoil your celebrations my friends, but my arms are aching badly. It is my turn to try."

Delano looked sympathetically and apologised as he ushered his friends out of the circle.

Once again the Bucca performed their strange ritual, passing King Maccus through the Men-an-Tol three times until lying him on the grass to wait for his healing. There was no dramatic silence or great thunder. The King just lay on the ground as the sun shone brightly around him. The grass, however, began to whisper and sigh as it gave up its pollen, which rose in huge swathes that surrounded King Maccus until he was totally out of sight from the rest. The great cloud of pollen circled him gently for a few moments in orange clouds and as quickly as it had risen around him it was gone again. King Maccus began moving his arms about as if he had never had arms before, with such joy and delight as he said, "I do not believe it. My bones were crushed and now they are rebuilt. I am cured!"

He sat laughing with delight, looking at his hands as if they belonged to someone else.

Tiernon approached Trahern the Bucca and shook him heartily by the shoulders as he spoke gratefully. "How can I ever repay your kindness my new friend?"

Trahern looked back at Tiernon with a look of great pride in his eyes. His answer was quick and without thought, "Take me with you."

Tiernon was astonished and did not know quite what to say as he looked at Delano for confirmation, which came easily. Delano simply nodded. Still a little choked by the offer Tiernon answered, "I will gladly take you with us. We need a strong man on our side and believe me, you are surely strong."

King Maccus was now on his feet. He had grown accustomed to having pain free arms and he joined in. "Take me with you. Fate has brought us together in strange circumstances. The Gods have brought us together and together we will succeed."

Once again Tiernon was overwhelmed and looked upon Delano for reassurance and once again, the wise Delano nodded as Tiernon said, "The greater our chances will be. Once we were five and now we are seven."

Trahern turned to Tiernon and said sternly, "It will soon be time to take you to the stone. It must become your burden. It is a heavy one, for the Evil One will feel its presence once it is on the move. We must sharpen our senses and never let it out of our sight from this day."

*

King Maccus agreed that the group should rest up at his fort for a few days to gather strength and take on sustenance. The journey to the West Mountains would be long and arduous; only a fool would attempt it whilst in such an ill-equipped disposition. Therefore for the next few days the group spent a happy time with their clansmen and the Bucca, together as comrades and all was well.

*

King Maccus informed his tribe that he was leaving the kingship to his eldest son whilst he was away. The clansmen were happy with his decision and proud that he was taking a role in the quest that they had heard so much about. The blacksmith forged King Maccus a new hammer with a head twice the size as the first and set it on a shaft that was twice the thickness and presented it to him. King Maccus held it aloft and spoke. "With my hammer I will crush any evil doer in the name of good."

Trahern also passed on his leadership to his brother. His people were equally as proud in the knowledge that he would play a part in the good quest and they too celebrated with elation. For the first time in many years one clan celebrated with another and creatures celebrated among men and they relished the camaraderie.

Chapter 12

The Seed of the Tree of Immortality

Tiernon and his comrades spent much of their time in the King's quarters laying down the best plan of action to reach the western mountains. It was decided unanimously that they would travel inland via strong ponies. Although sailing around the coast would be much faster, it would leave them at the mercy of mermaids and Kelpies.

King Maccus ordered his blacksmith to make a new sword for Kael and requested that it be the finest in the land. The blacksmith decorated the hilt with the figure of a dragon encircled by its tail. At the end of the hilt was a hollow iron circle. This was an unusual engraving for a Celtic sword but it represented the battle against the swamp dragon and the healing at the Men-an-Tol. Kael was overwhelmed when the blacksmith presented him with the sword and he said humbly, "I thank you, kind Sir. I hope I can honour such a fine gift."

He swished the sword around wildly as he admired the light that reflected from the shiny blade before setting it to rest in its scabbard.

Breanna was pleased for her brother and she smiled sweetly towards him as she said, "Welcome back, Kael. Never again will I let you out of my sight. I swear from this day that I will let no harm befall you again."

Vaughan smiled to himself as he watched the two siblings talking together. He remembered their younger years when they would quibble over the most nonsensical matters and felt a great privilege to witness their bonds growing stronger.

Trahern beckoned to Tiernon, "I think it is a good time for my people to return to our land. I will take you to the stone but no one else must witness the secret place. I suggest the rest of you wait here for our return."

Tiernon looked in bewilderment as he asked, "Is that necessary? You are among friends."

Trahern thoughtfully replied, "I do not wish to insult anyone but who knows what may happen. I want to keep the hiding place a total secret. Should disaster strike at least I might have the chance of returning the stone back to hiding, lest your quest fail."

Tiernon gave a look of respect as he replied, "That is a wise decision. I agree. We shall go at once. The rest of you enjoy the hospitality whilst we are gone for when we return you must be ready to leave."

The Bucca said their goodbyes to their newfound friends. It was a sad occasion for some and there was lots of hugging and shedding of tears.

Tiernon set off with Trahern on two strong ponies. The Bucca tribe made their way on foot and before long the two horsemen were a long way ahead and soon reached the mines.

Trahern was the first to dismount and scurried off through an entrance that Tiernon had not seen before. He found it difficult to squeeze through as it was not intended for full-grown men. The entrance led to a narrow tunnel that was uneven with jagged walls. The pair had to travel slowly to avoid injury as they ventured deeper into the earth until coming to an open chamber that was lit by flaming torches.

Once Tiernon's eyes adjusted to the light he was dumfounded by the mountain of treasures that were heaped about the floor. Precious stones such as jade, jet and emeralds were intertwined amongst the pile of riches and among the alcoves Tiernon could see that they were bulging with trinkets that had been crafted skilfully by the Bucca. He saw diamonds the size of his fist scattered about the place and marvelled at the collection of silver and gold cups. He picked up the biggest and most decorated cup and said to Trahern. "The stone must be of equal beauty to these treasures that you protect."

Trahern shook his head in disappointment as he spoke, "You do not fully comprehend the magnitude of the sacred stone seed. Its beauty lies in the Creator. It is worth more than all our treasures. Come I will show you."

He led Tiernon into the darkest corner of the chamber and reached inside the furthest hole. Stretching his arm inside, he scratched about for a moment until emerging with a large but unobtrusive wooden box, which he quickly passed to Tiernon as he said, "This box must never be opened outside of this cave. Go ahead and look."

Tiernon held the box tightly in anticipation. He tried to imagine how shiny the seed would gleam and how many jewels would adorn it. He teased the lid slightly open peering inside the crack, almost hesitating to open the box until finding the courage to allow the lid to swing fully open. To his astonishment he saw a very unattractive, smooth stone ball, surprisingly ample in size needing two hands to hold it. Tiernon noticed that the stone had writing etched into it that he could not comprehend. Unbeknown to him the writing was ancient, written with the very hand of the Creator. It was in a language unknown to earth kind, planted into the physiology of every seed from the Tree of Life with instructions of how to nurture and care for the seed.

The language was only comprehendible to the Creator and to the Evil One and therefore Tiernon was suspicious of the stone ball. He could not hide his contempt as he spoke sharply to Trahern,

"What kind of trickery is this? You present me with a poorly written carved stone with no significant power or majesty."

Trahern responded fearfully, "Mind your manners and show some reverence. This stone is a symbol of all hope and the saviour of mankind. Only an evil, greedy race would expect it to be of great finery, that is why it has remained hidden so well amongst the gold and riches. The stone holds more power than the Men-an-Tol. It has the power of great good. The sooner you understand that the more capable you will be at protecting it. It is good that your eyes perceive the seed as a meagre stone. It would be wise to call it a stone outside of these walls to protect its identity from prying eyes and open ears."

Tiernon was humbled by Trahern's speech and admired his tenaciousness. He quickly apologised and Trahern spoke on, "I have seen what you have seen as do all the guardians of the stone, but many have failed in the past because they could not understand the significance. Before I can pass this burden to you I must ask the question, who do you serve?"

Tiernon's eyes burned with the fire of passion as he realised his mistake. His thoughts passed to the time when he met his Creator. The moment had come for Tiernon to put a lifelong commitment behind him and turn his back on a culture which was instilled in him since birth. He knew he had to take his secret to his grave and never tell a soul of the future prophecy, so he thought long and hard before answering.

When he found the strength to answer it was difficult and painful, but it flowed from his lips like wine from a jar. "I serve the Creator".

Trahern was elated as the answer was both wise and correct and he patted Tiernon sternly on the back as he said, "You are ready my friend. You are not alone for I will help you and share your burden. I too have witnessed the suffering of my people for the protection of the stone. That is why I am bound to travel with you until you find the strength to acknowledge the truth without question."

Tiernon replaced the stone safely within the box and wrapped it carefully within his beloved White Bear banner.

The pair made their way back to the waiting ponies and set a blistering pace towards the fort of the Dumnonii. On the way they were greeted by the returning Bucca and Trahern halted his mount as he spoke to his people, "Farewell my friends and family, I may not return but my thoughts are with you. I will rest assured on my travels that you are now free from your toil. May you all live out your lives in peace and happiness."

A woman and a young boy bustled their way to the front of the crowd. Both had sorrow on their faces and their eyes were filled with tears to the brink of bursting. The woman hugged Trahern by the leg as his pony dithered back and forth and she sobbed to him, "Take care, my love. I will wait a lifetime for your return and never forget you."

The small boy joined in the hugging, clearly distraught as he spoke, "Nor I father, I will never forget you."

Trahern dismounted and joined his family for some brief hugging and kissing before taking a deep breath and returning to his pony. He could no longer find any words so he set off with a token wave and did not look back for his heart was heavy.

The duo continued onwards but the atmosphere was very sombre. Trahern travelled silently as he battled with his thoughts of whether he would ever see his loved ones again.

*

The sun was low in the sky before they reached the fort of the Dumnonii. The gates were swung open and Delano was the first to greet them and questioned Tiernon as he dismounted from his pony, "Have you got the stone in your possession?"

Tiernon responded quietly, "I have indeed, but I have been warned that it must never see the light of day whilst it is in my possession. I am afraid I cannot reveal it to you."

Delano was a little dismayed but hid his disappointment as he replied, "Do not fear old friend, I do not need to see it. I am honoured enough to be part of your company. When are we to leave for the West Mountains?"

"We must leave at first light," Tiernon replied.

*

Early the next day the seven comrades saddled their ponies, laden with travel sacks full of essentials and set off towards the Western Mountains.

Chapter 13

The Brigantes Flee from Cythrawl

King Alfred thus far had done a wonderful job keeping the Brigantes tribes of the Northern Province from internal squabbling and as a result they prospered well in their lands. Crops were good and animal yield was profound, but this was no surprise to the Brigantes since Alfred's prowess as a wonderful leader was known to all.

Alfred was a great fighter and ruled his kingdom with discipline, ensuring that all fit men and women trained for battle on a regular basis. Everybody was used to habitual training and no one seemed to notice that the training calls to arms and early morning drills were becoming more and more frequent.

Alfred had spent almost every night of late in restless bouts of sweat filled dreaming; pacing about his quarters, checking for would be assassins, tormented by paranoia that he could be killed at any moment. This behaviour was unusual for such a great man but Alfred was troubled with dreams of a great frenzied attack from enemies filled with hatred and great powers, assisted by the Evil One, in attempts to dislodge the Brigantes Clans.

He was normally a strong-minded person and would usually bear such a burden alone but he was at the end of his tether. He woke early one morning after a bout of insomnia and made his way to the fort gates, demanding to the lookout rather rudely and sharply that the gates be opened. The lookout responded without hesitation as he knew that the King was vexed.

Alfred headed towards the river that ran from the north and began chanting in an old tongue as Tiernon had showed him and beckoned Shylah, who appeared as beautiful as ever. But her face was troubled as she rose gracefully from the depths of the water.

"What can I do for you?" she asked kindly.

Alfred looked at her woefully as he replied, "My dreams are filled with pain. I cannot sleep for I fear we are going to come under attack. I wonder if you could shed any light as to what it all means."

Shylah bowed her head in acknowledgement as she answered solemnly, "I am afraid that your dreams are founded on truth, for I have seen what will transpire. The Evil One has corrupted the northern Parissi of the Wolds and convinced them to join forces with our enemies from the southern clans. They are plotting together to journey into our land and attack us from both sides in a cowardly siege."

King Alfred was angered by such dishonourable behaviour and so he scorned, "It is a disgrace that a tribe can contemplate skulking to battle unannounced in the night. Why would they do such a thing?"

Shylah paused in thought for a moment before giving her reply, "The Evil One fears that the chosen are much further into their quest than anyone thought possible and so he intends to obliterate the very people that the chosen are trying to save."

King Alfred was horrified by the thought of it and questioned Shylah further, "When will this abomination take place? Can you tell me if there is a way that we can outsmart them?"

Shylah gave Alfred a look of uncertainty as she answered, "I cannot tell you when this attack will take place, for evil magic is at work against my powers of insight. I do know that you must gather all your people and their belongings and journey north. A force more powerful than any army is also coming for you. The Evil One has conjured Cythrawl, the great nothing."

King Alfred was physically trembling for he knew too well the old tales of Cythrawl, which was created at the beginning of time from chaos; a great black hole which could be conjured to earth to devour everything into its bottomless void. So he listened intently as Shylah continued with her prophecy, "You must head northwards and follow your heart, for you will know the way. You must push on and take only brief respite until you have found safe haven. Cythrawl has limited time on earth and your saving grace is avoidance so you must set off at first light, for time is not on your side. That is all I can tell you."

Shylah sank into the depths of the water as she spoke in dismay, "make haste, King Alfred. Leave immediately."

And she was gone.

*

The next day Alfred summoned his nobles to council. Unable to find the right words to say, he thought his best option would be the truth and so he came right out and told them that Cythrawl was coming. His nobles began quivering in their seats.

The King had a hard time calming the nobles but eventually managed to restore order. Many questions were asked but the King had no answers, yet eventually it was decided for each noble to tell his subjects the truth and make ready for evacuation.

*

Farmers loaded their carts with cages containing piglets and hens. Drovers gathered flocks of geese, pigs and goats as equestrians rounded up the cattle and brown sheep. Willow was gathered in great lengths for building temporary fencing on the journey. Huge sheets of buckskin were loaded for the use of temporary shelter. Foot soldiers flanked the great exodus of people, and the cavalry took the lead. King Alfred held aloft his hand once everyone was ready and beckoned to them.

"Let us proceed. We must take it slowly, we do not wish to lose anyone on the way. Be aware of your neighbour, be selfless and vigilant and look out for each other." With that said they progressed slowly northward and away from their homes.

The drovers were adept with the walking poultry and livestock, keeping a brisk pace and the people on the heavy carts ambled behind on the uneven tracks to the sound of their wheels groaning with the load.

They travelled onwards making steady progress as the foot soldiers marched beside them, watching intently for any danger. The air was filled with anxiety as no one could relax with the thought that Cythrawl was on their heels and they journeyed steadily on until the daylight hours had almost faded. Their pace was not swift but they had managed to put twenty miles between them and the fort.

*

The next morning the travellers began packing away their buckskin tents from the previous night's vigil, gathering their livestock, completely unaware that Cythrawl was already making slow yet steady progress towards their abandoned fort. Animals fled from the nearby forest with wide eyes and flocks of birds flew noisily to safety as Cythrawl crept like a dark blanket out of the forest, consuming everything in its path. Trees groaned loudly as they crashed to earth, plants were trampled by invisible forces as they succumbed to the darkness and were scooped up by a vacuum of nothing. Cythrawl crept meticulously on until reaching the fort gates of the lower hill dwellings, which came crashing down along with the walls and buildings as they disappeared amongst the darkness. The dark matter continued through the villages consuming all in its path until reaching the main fort at the top of the hill, taking with it every wall, fence, building and plant. The destruction left behind was immense; not a blade of grass or stone was left behind except for a huge void in the earth where once there was land.

*

The Brigantes Clan was well into their second day of hard travelling. Their spirits were lifted by singing along the way, travelling with intent through the open plains and marshes towards the north. King Alfred ordered the group with precision and followed his instinct towards unknown territory. They were heading towards the borders of Brigantes, where no other Brigantes had been before. He maintained a northward approach until his conscience pricked him to follow a north-easterly path.

One of the carts ambled along precariously near the edge of a steep banking until it lost tracking and plunged into the valley below, laden with vital supplies and clansmen. A rescue attempt ensued. The foot soldiers tethered ropes to strong trees that lined the pathway and abseiled down the steep valley. They rescued a family with small children and livestock, carrying them up the hill one by one. The cart was the hardest to bring up. It was not damaged so the soldiers righted it back on to four wheels and tethered it to three strong ponies that were whipped until they pulled on the ropes. The weight of the cart buckled their legs as they struggled to get a footing on the loose ground. Eventually they found their feet and were able to pull the cart back to the top. The family was elated. They loaded their cart with their livestock and belongings as quickly as possible and were soon on their way again.

The day passed all too quickly, the incident had cost them much time; they had only managed to travel about ten miles.

Hunger was a major factor and many small fires sprouted up about the area as families began cooking their animals.

*

As the night sky darkened Cythrawl maintained its steady course towards the travellers, never stopping for rest or sleep. It had closed the gap whilst the Brigantes struggled to rescue their comrades and continued to close in whilst they slept, leaving a trail of withered land behind it that subsided into the chasm. These were the tracks of Cythrawl. The darkness of Cythrawl crawled mercilessly forward through the marsh, taking with it small amphibious creatures, fish and even the water, leaving dry patches of land and huge ditches where the water once flowed.

*

The next day the Brigantes broke camp and trundled onwards following the great King Alfred. The people were now becoming weary, but they picked up their pace all the same as they could sense that Cythrawl was closing in on them. They eventually arrived at a large forest that was untouched by man's hand. This was a lush forest and had an air about it that put a smile on the faces of all who entered. Trees sprawled out towards the sunlight growing tall and strong. Holly grew beneath great oak trees and brambles crept along the ground in thickets. This was no ordinary forest; it was filled with magic and fairy folk.

King Alfred and his people were making good progress, when suddenly from behind them animals and fairy folk alike bolted in great herds as if chased by an invisible hunter. Birds flew in all directions chattering loudly. They were so blinded by fear that they overtook the travellers rapidly and paid no heed to their presence, disappearing deep into the forest ahead.

The Brigantes halted for a moment and an uneasy murmur sounded around the people, which was abruptly interrupted by the groaning of a large oak that fell to the ground behind them. As the travellers looked in the direction of the fallen tree, they saw with fear the great darkness of Cythrawl consuming all life in its path and in a blind panic they ran as fast as they could.

The exodus of people whipped their carts into action as foot soldiers ran and cavalry soldiers rode like the wind. The drovers no longer needed to push their brown sheep and geese forward, for they were off as fast as their legs could take them amidst a cacophony of baying and gaggling. The cattle stampeded away from the darkness, taking any direction possible in order to evade the dark death. Cythrawl increased in speed as it could sense that it was close to its goal and chased the exhausted clansmen and women, consuming all the trees and bushes, leaving a great scar in the forest behind it.

King Alfred eventually rose to his responsibility as a leader, fighting his fear as he turned his mount around and headed back to his people. He gathered some soldiers who reluctantly followed and proceeded to help the stragglers that were falling behind, loading them on to carts.

Cythrawl was breathing down their necks as they journeyed deeper and deeper into the enchanted forest. The trees grew closer together and the undergrowth became denser, slowing their progress to a near standstill as soldiers hacked at the forest with their swords in attempts to make a pathway.

King Alfred ordered a group of his bravest warriors to form a human shield between Cythrawl and his people and with swords aloft and spears at the ready, they waited for Cythrawl to come. They gathered in a line behind a huge oak tree that grew tall and fat with its branches sprawled outwards low to the ground.

Cythrawl was upon them and in the darkness the King could see the trees and plants swirling around in the abyss as they disappeared into nothing. He could hear the rumble of wind as it swirled within the black chasm like a gigantic vacuum. His men trembled as it crept closer and the King shouted as the wind swirled about him. "HOLD! Do not leave your post. We will die as heroes this day, not cowards."

The loyal soldiers held their nerve as sweat dripped from their brows and their hands trembled about their swords. Cythrawl was but inches away when suddenly it ground to a halt, crashing against an unseen barrier like sea waves crashing against rocks. Cythrawl backed up and made another attempt to break the unseen barrier and the dark mass rose up like a black tidal wave in front of the petrified King and his soldiers. The huge oak tree that they were sheltered behind suddenly glowed with the intensity of the sun and to the astonishment of everyone present, the tree spoke. "Cythrawl of the old world, your place is not for this earth. Your place is of the universe and your food is the stars. Be gone I command thee. Be gone."

Cythrawl responded with a huge groan as it tried continuously to break the unseen force field. The oak burned brighter still and the tree spoke on. "Get back. I command thee get back, for I am the Green Man. I will smite thee with my powers and you will feel my wrath."

Cythrawl groaned again and the Green Man continued. "You have no sway over me on Earth, you belong amongst the planets. Now be gone."

The Green Man set a gigantic shockwave of energy from his trunk that projected through the energy field and into Cythrawl as he chanted in an ancient language. He was casting a spell on Cythrawl that was a reverse of the evil spell used to conjure it. His chanting became louder and Cythrawl's groans turned to earth shattering screams as it formed a huge swirling ball that circled aggressively, like an angry swarm of bees, before hurtling headlong towards the open sky and into space from whence it came.

King Alfred and his soldiers cheered and were overwhelmed by their saviour. The mayhem subsided and people began gathering themselves around the great oak tree and knelt in honour of the Green Man.

King Alfred turned to look at the oak and he saw the great face of the Green Man protruding from its trunk.

The Green Man was a legend amongst the Celts. Many questioned his existence for it was said that his spirit was older than the earth itself. As the King stared in bewilderment he realised that this must be true for the Green Man's face was etched with cracks and gnarls that ran long and deep. His skin had the texture and colour of the oak itself and his hair hung about his face like leaves on thin branches. His eye lids were heavy and wrinkled, drooping low around his yellow eyes which gave away his great age, yet they glowed with a softness that was comforting.

The Green Man, although appearing within the oak, was not actually a tree. He was a powerful spirit that could appear in any tree, in any forest, at any time, but he preferred the oak. He blinked a few times and spoke in a deep low tone to the King, "Worthy King Alfred, you have followed wisely the instructions of the great Shylah. Your courage has become your saving grace and now you must heed my words."

King Alfred rose from bended knee to listen to the Green Man as he spoke on.

"You are to lead your people northwards for two days until you come to the land of the hills. Your journey will become harder, eventually leading you to a colossal escarpment growing in a semi-circle from the hills. This rocky outcrop will seem impossible to climb but you must travel around it until you come to a steep incline.

You must climb to the top of the escarpment where the land flattens and there you must build a fortress. This will take your people many weeks of hard toil and labour, but it is only on Roulston Scar that your people will be safe from the tribes that are to come."

King Alfred questioned the Green Man intently, "How will we fight the tribes that are to come? I understand there will be many."

The Green Man replied in earnest, "You must build ramparts of wood higher than the tallest man, around the whole perimeter and dig deep ditches that are not easy to cross. Do not waste your time building homes; make temporary dwellings. If you heed my words you will be able to stave off the largest army with a few good soldiers."

King Alfred replied humbly, "I thank you for your kind advice. I am deeply in your debt."

The Green Man answered with a smile, "I will bide you some time. I will send a great storm to the southern tribes and the Parissi of the Wolds. I will blow down their camps and chase away their livestock."

*

The Green Man disappeared without warning. His gnarled face melted into the great oak and he was gone, but his voice rang out from where he had faded. "Heed my words, oh King. Follow your heart for I am with it. Follow your head for I am in it. Follow your plan for I have given it to you. Do this and the battle shall be won and you will not have to draw a single sword."

*

The Brigantes sprang into action, gathering as many of their stray animals as they could muster until night fell yet again. The next morning they were all up and about packing their belongings on to their carts and the journey to Roulston Scar began.

For two days and nights the group ventured north, guided by King Alfred as they reached the hill country that the Green Man had foretold but nothing prepared them for the site of Roulston Scar, for it sprouted out of the ground towards the sky, dwarfing all the land and trees around it. The cliff face was sheer, shooting almost straight upwards in a semi-circle. A few bushes and trees hung precariously from its ledges. It seemed impregnable but King Alfred remembered the Green Man's advice and led his people to the other side, where they were met with a thickly forested embankment that climed steeply to the top of the mountain. The journey to the top was long and hard as the trees severely hindered their progress, yet eventually they reached the summit where the land was bare of trees and the grasses ruled. The platform was vast and flat and the view from the top ran as far as the eye could see. King Alfred dismounted from his pony and turned to his people, "We will take a rest and make camp and feed well today, but tomorrow we must begin our work."

He then summoned his council and lay well thought out plans for how they would build a fortress. His council agreed and disagreed at the best course of action until they all decided on the best plans.

*

The next day work began and one group of workers set about clearing the trees from around the top of the steep slope. The wood was used to build temporary living quarters for both man and beast. Farmers began making sections of the plateaux ready for planting crops and used their huge oxen to plough the soil whilst the women and children weeded out the long grasses.

The first stage in their plan took more than a week but eventually they had created a reasonable village with neat, wooden buildings that perched precariously on wooden stilts. The next stage was much more difficult as they collected rocks from the surrounding woodland below, dragging them up the steep slope with ox and cart, using the rocks to build walls around the entire perimeter that stood six feet high and six feet wide, leaving two openings at strategic points in the fortress. This was heavy and painstaking work which took the clan at least a moon's cycle to complete. The third stage was to clear more trees from the slope, using them to build a box rampart on top of the stone wall, fronted by a timber palisade that stood almost nine feet tall in places. The palisade was built from straight sturdy logs set deep in the ground and the tops were fashioned into sharpened points.

King Alfred was still not satisfied with his fortress and ordered his people to dig wide ditches around the perimeter, making the fence appear even higher from the outside and impossible to climb. This task took another moon's cycle to complete, but eventually the fortress was ready and finally he posted soldiers around the perimeter on the box ramparts in constant vigil for danger. At last, the clan could settle down to normality. The slope was now almost bare of trees and the view from the ramparts was good. Anyone within forty miles could easily be seen. This was the most formidable fort ever built.

Chapter 14

Hogarth the Red Dragon

Tiernon and his band of friends had made extremely good progress along the rough terrain on their sturdy ponies and arrived, without any major incidents in the land of the western mountains. Kael spied the first mountain in the area and turned to Breanna jesting. "I can see why they call it the land of the mountains."

Breanna giggled. "Yes, and to think we have to climb them!"

The thought of hard climbing had not previously occurred to Kael so he screwed up his face in displeasure as Vaughan gestured to him, "I do not think that these beasts will make it. Perhaps we will have to walk."

Delano turned to Tiernon in agreement, "I think that Vaughan may be right. From here some of those peaks seem deadly on foot, never mind on beast."

Tiernon nodded towards the group, "It is a sad fact. We will ride as long as we can, but alas, at some point we must proceed on foot."

King Maccus turned to Trahern, the Bucca. "That will not be sorry news for you my friend. I know how fond you are of riding."

Trahern would relish the thought of walking as he hated his pony, for it had caused him much discomfort on the journey with its unruly behaviour towards him.

"Be glad to see the back of it. I might even eat the cursed creature." He replied with a grin.

The group erupted in laughter at the thought of Trahern eating his pony, for they had witnessed the many times that it had refused to move a muscle and the time it threw Trahern into the river because it did not want to cross it.

Tiernon stared carefully at the landscape. He had travelled this way on many previous adventures with Delano. He knew well the lair of the red dragon of the *Yr Wyddfa* Mountain, the dragon's barrow. The *Yr Wyddfa* Mountain was the chosen burial ground of the ancient dragons in the times when the large beasts dominated the earth. Tiernon had a good knowledge of the land beyond where the mountains gave way to the valleys and in turn, to the woodlands and hills. It was with this in mind that he made a decision and spoke with his colleagues. "I think it would be a detriment to our journey to lose the ponies at this stage. I would like a volunteer to travel around the rocky region along the lower grounds to the northeast side and wait for us there."

Tiernon looked towards Delano as he spoke knowing full well that he alone had good knowledge of the lands. Delano knew how to take a hint, so he nodded. "I will travel as a horse and lead the ponies to the other side of Mount *Yr Wyddfa*. I will see you there."

Without hesitation he transformed, gathered the ponies and was on his way. Tiernon and the rest of his band made their way slowly through the valley towards the ever-looming Mount *Yr Wyddfa* that became more ominous the closer that they approached.

As Breanna browsed the open blue sky, she was positive that she could see a large, red bird soaring on effortless wings in and out of the strong sunlight, but she could never get a good enough look as the sun hurt her eyes. She pointed it out to Kael, who struggled to see it for himself, apart from fleeting glimpses. The beast was camouflaged from the eye. Trahern, the Bucca, walked happily, grateful to be rid of his cursed mount for the time being.

King Maccus followed closely behind Vaughan, using his huge hammer as a walking stick. Tiernon noticed the children's constant staring towards the sun and looked for himself. He too noticed the beast flitting in and out of the sun and knew instantly that it was Hogarth, the red dragon. He smiled to himself at the thought of meeting a very old friend once again. The group eventually came to a valley that led the way gradually up the mountain. Tiernon chose this route because he knew the climb would be safer for the children and so the group walked the steady incline across the dark flinty paths towards the peak. They got their first glimpse of a large glacial lake that popped in and out of view as they climbed and as they got higher they saw the lake in all its glory with its clear blue waters glistening in the crisp sunlight. Vaughan was in awe.

The climb became a little more difficult and the group found that they were becoming more reliant on both their hands and feet. King Maccus was forced to carry his hammer in its sling on his back and everyone was now treading lightly and skilfully towards the peak.

On they clambered until the land flattened out, giving a short respite, but the group soon found themselves facing a very narrow precipice with a large slope on one side and a sheer drop on the other, which offered no hand holds.

*

The group was forced to travel single file, and no-one spoke a word; self-preservation was at the forefront of everybody's mind. Even Trahern, the seasoned excavator of mines and deep shafts, was awed by the sheer drop on either side.

Once over this obstacle the ground opened out toward a flat plateau and the group was able to spread out. From here on the climb was much easier and became a simple amble to the very top. Breanna stared at the sun as the large circling beast became ever clearer to her and she saw for the first time the beautiful red dragon, gliding on delicate wings that were transparent enough to see the dragon's veins, which spread out towards the tips. The dragon trailed its back legs whilst it tucked its front legs into the chest. Breanna could now see that the dragon had two large horns growing out of its head and had whiskers that grew in long straggles out from its chin and eyebrows. Breanna knew it was a dragon because it had a fierce glare. It did not look as if it was friendly to her.

The group was soon at the summit and they sat at the top waiting for the dragon to come to them. It flew high and then low, in sight then out of sight, until suddenly it landed with a loud thud. Kael fell backwards and Vaughan trembled. He was sure the dragon would eat them, as he had never encountered a good dragon. King Maccus reached for his hammer, but his friend Trahern, gestured for him not to and Tiernon bowed.

Hogarth the dragon spoke to Tiernon. "I trusted that you would make the right choice in this matter and am happy that you showed great courage and honour to get this far. I know the pain endured when carrying such a burden. Show me the stone that you protect and I shall show you the way to your new Kingdom."

Tiernon carefully pulled out the large wooden box containing the carved stone and offered it to Hogarth. Without inspection, Hogarth grasped it in his huge, clawed hand and took to the air with a single leap and strong wing beats. He disappeared for a few moments and returned empty handed. The stone seed was safely hidden until a time when it could be returned to the Creator.

Hogarth addressed the group. "You must travel to the district of the lakes and mountains. From there you will be able to follow the way to the chosen lands where you will build a new kingdom."

Hogarth gave a piece of parchment to Tiernon who quickly shoved it into his tunic for safe keeping. Tiernon spoke to Hogarth with his power of telepathy. "My oldest friend, I trust that if you are involved in this endeavour, then my choice to see this through must be a wise one."

Hogarth was troubled by these words and replied with the power of his mind, "The time for Druids and dragons is nearly at an end, but the Creator will remember our deeds and take us to his Kingdom at the end of ages because we believe the unbelievable. We accept the unacceptable and because the Creator commands it, we leave behind everything that we thought was dear to us."

Tiernon was moved by the speech and his eyes welled up as he placed his hand on his heart. "True is your friendship and wise are your words. Until we meet again, old friend."

Hogarth beat his wings rapidly and leapt to the air at great speed, circling until catching the best thermal that took him high into the clouds before disappearing into the distance.

*

The group made their way to the other side of *Yr Wyddfar*, where they were met by Delano. Tiernon wasted no time scrutinising the parchment as soon as the group were reunited. He took it from his tunic with a wry smile in expectancy of a great revelation, but the smile fell away from his face as he unrolled the parchment. Delano was the first to notice his dismay and asked. "What is it?"

Tiernon showed Delano the parchment and Delano read it aloud. "Travel to the North until the land you tread is unknown to you. Then, where Draco once ruled, you will see in the darkness the great white bear and her cub. You must follow the mother bear and her cub as she roams the heavens. She watches over her shoulder and keeps an eye on her playful youngster. Look over her shoulder till you see the cub's tail and follow that trail, for that will lead you to the burial place of the White Bear talisman and the Promised Land where the Celtic line will never cease."

Delano almost scrunched the parchment in frustration and he questioned, "What is this riddle? It is utter nonsense."

King Maccus interrupted sharply, "Is that it? Is that the payment we receive for risking life and limb?

The Bucca and Vaughan stood silent for a moment, for they were creatures of an older race than Delano and their race and line were older than Tiernon. The ways of their people passed down stories through each generation to the next to keep tradition and memory alive.

Trahern spoke out. "During the great ice age, Draco the Dragon ruled the celestial sky and paved the way for early man to navigate the world. He was steadfast at his post until one day his leadership was challenged when he met with a protective mother and her cub."

Suddenly, Vaughan gave a sigh of recognition and Trahern gave him leave to continue, so Vaughan began to tell the rest of the tale. "The story tells of a great battle in the sky, so fierce that the earth moved from its position and almost plummeted out of the universe, but Draco the Dragon chased it and stopped it, causing the Earth to spin, but in doing so Draco lost his throne."

Vaughan glanced at Trahern. "I am unsure of the rest."

Trahern continued the rest of the story, "Draco the Dragon lost his throne saving the earth from falling. This meant that Draco the Dragon no longer held the North position. The ancient civilisations studied the position of Draco and realised he pointed true North, but after the battle when the earth was moved, his position seemed to shift and the great white bear now points the way north through her cub's tail."

Vaughan was grinning from ear to ear and Trahern too, but still the group did not understand. They looked at each other in dismay and then as he looked up towards the sky, Vaughan explained. "The journey's directions are in the night sky. It is the stars that we are supposed to follow, at night when they are clear to light the way north."

Tiernon doubled over with laughter at the sheer simplicity of the riddle as he guffawed. "Of course, Polaris the North Star, Ursa Major the Great White Bear and Ursa Minor the cub. I should have known."

At last everyone gathered themselves together to venture on with their quest. As they all resumed their trusty mounts, Trahern's all knowing smile turned to dismay when he realised that he must ride the pony with a mind of its own for heaven knows how many days. They set off in the direction of the lands of the mountains and lakes.

*

Tiernon and Delano knew the direction well for they had ventured that way on many a battle, but the land beyond was unknown to them. The twins chatted to Vaughan about the meeting with Hogarth. However brief it was, they would never forget it. Vaughan was of the conviction that there was no such thing as a good dragon. King Maccus, overwhelmed by the meeting, said very little in the days that followed. Therefore the group travelled on towards their goal with hope and victory in sight, unaware that their clansmen were held up at Roulstan Scar, awaiting battle.

Chapter 15

The Battle at Roulston Scar

King Alfred, never satisfied with his ever-growing fortress, had his soldiers laying traps around the lower slopes made from trees that were chopped down and then propped precariously upright again, leaning loosely against neighbouring trees. He had them do this every hundred feet or so, from the very bottom of the slopes to the halfway point. He also had his men unearth great boulders from the ground and drag them to within a few feet of the perimeter fence. He had the boulders rested on mounds of small stones and on many occasions the boulders threatened to roll down the hill on their own accord, so steeply were they leaning. The men had wedged huge, wooden shafts underneath the stones so that they could be teased to fall in a controlled direction when the time was right.

Alfred was still unsatisfied with the security of his fortress. He ordered his men to slaughter and kill half the pigs in the camp. He had them all painstakingly roasted on hot burning spits and collected all the melted fat from the carcasses. This was hungry work but worth it. By the end of the week the people were growing tired of pork.

In the meantime he had people foraging the woods, collecting beeswax and in the field, he had farmers collecting seeds for pressing into oil.

His men had to dig deep pits around the slope then each pit was filled to the brim with dry wood and a mixture of melted pig fat, beeswax and seed oil was poured in. Alfred had his men dig channels and fill them with dry timber and the pig fat mixture. The intertwining channels connected each pit until resting at the perimeter of the fortress just outside the main gate.

At last King Alfred felt that they were ready for the battle to come. And come it did!

*

As Shylah had predicted the Parissi and the collective clans from the southern tribes made their way steadily towards the great escarpment under cover of the night hours. King Alfred's lookouts kept constant communications with the runners on the proximity of the marchers, keeping a constant tally. The numbers were rising all the time until it was estimated that there must be an army of around ten thousand strong. The runners took turns to inform the council until the time approached for the King to make his first move.

Alfred waited until the marching army was about six miles away and he ordered the drill horn to be blown, reminding his people to take arms and be ready at their set posts.

Everything was planned to the last detail and everyone knew their place and what they must do. Firstly, all the animals, children and elderly were moved to the central huts of the fortress for safety. Then, every able-bodied man, woman and child of teenage years painted their blue war paint on to their faces and those that had manufactured strong armour quickly dressed accordingly. The best bowmen and women amongst them did something never seen before in a Celtic battle. They took their place at the perimeter walls with bows at the ready to fire upon the marching army as they made their way up the hill.

*

Chariots were loaded with the dry wood, pig fat, wax and oil mixture and pushed out of the gates, forming a barrier between the slope and the exterior.

It was now a waiting game and the Brigantes waited in total darkness for over an hour, but it seemed much longer as the tension squeezed the air tighter than a bear's head in a honeybee nest.

To the approaching army it must have seemed as if they were sneaking up on to their enemy, such was the quietness of the Brigantes.

The waiting heroes could now hear loud voices as the massive army drew nearer through the thick forest and the dark night carried conversations to the ears of the waiting party, conversations of how the men below were going to butcher and torture and burn.

*

King Alfred gave the command to a young boy to sneak out over the open drawbridge and set alight the channel filled with the dry timber and fat mixture at the front of the gate. The boy quietly crept out and lit the channel which set ablaze instantly, so expertly done was the drying of the timber. The flames burnt within the hidden walls of earth. Although the oncoming army could now see a flickering light coming from the fortress, it was not apparent that it was a raging fire making headway towards them. They kept on coming with a confidence that was rapidly spreading and growing.

Eventually, the swarm of warriors reached the lower part of the slope until suddenly from many different places, the waiting Brigantes could hear the groaning of large timber trees falling and the wailing of many men as they were crushed by the timber traps below. Time and time again groaning of trees and wailing of many men dying beneath their weight reached the ears of the Brigantes through the darkness, but still the vast army came ever closer.

*

Suddenly and violently the darkness gave way to blazing orange lights that roared down the hill in all directions from the pits that were filled with dry timber and pig fat. The channels, which had burned away slowly within the secrecy of the high pit walls, had reached shearing temperatures due to the melting pig fat mixture and once that caught alight there was no escape, for it exploded into infernos all around the slope. The bowmen who stood on top of the ramparts suddenly got a great view of the oncoming army as the flames lit the whole area. They could see soldiers writhing in agony as fires engulfed their whole bodies, screaming in horrid fits until the flames consumed them. King Alfred had timed his plan perfectly as almost half the oncoming army were now halfway up the steep slope and were engulfed in flames every which way, with nowhere to run but back down the slope. Unfortunately for them the wind followed them down the slope and fed the fires, setting light to the trees left standing and the flames chased the army wherever they went. Most of the fleeing army were either burnt by incinerating fire or crushed by falling trees. It was a massacre of outstanding proportions and the Brigantes had not drawn a single sword.

*

The warriors who escaped the flames and falling trees fled to the lower forest and set up camp where they stayed for the next few days. The slope raged in fire for days following the battle as the fat mixture reached shearing temperatures and refused to go out. Hunger took its toll as the army came ill-equipped; they had not expected to come across such an organised assault.

*

141

King Alfred sent out a small troop of men to scan the area once the fires had almost burnt out. The steep slope was almost bare and it made for a great advantage for the Brigantes. But this was no coincidence, it was simply part of the plan of the greatest tactician that ever lived and Alfred expected the report that came back to him. He was not surprised to learn that the army was camped up two miles to the southeast, in the forest below.

*

The battle horn blew once more and King Alfred sprang his men into action. They waited once again in silence as the oncoming mass made their way up the slope.

Confident with his plan, Alfred led a band of warriors out of the fortress gate, even leaving the gate open as they watched the army scrabble up the steep slope towards them. Although their army had dwindled to half their numbers, it was still a very large mass of soldiers that made their way towards camp. Alfred waited steadfast and steely-eyed as he watched the army climb closer until they were just beyond the halfway point. It was only then that King Alfred signalled the horn blower to make his call. At the sound of the horn the kings men set fire to the chariots filled with the dry timber and pig fat mixture and systematically rolled each one down the hill towards the frightened and debilitated army. Men, women and young boys who were just old enough to fight ran in all directions to avoid the burning chariots which were falling and rolling, spilling hot flames of wood and burning pig fat down the slope towards the fleeing army. King Alfred ordered his men to set loose the boulders that were propped precariously on the small rocks and they plundered down the slopes crushing all in their path. Some collided with the burning chariots, sending flames and burning fat that chased the soldiers down the slope. The sound of death resonated all around. A cacophony of screams and wails could be heard as the dying and injured were either set a light or crushed by rocks. Some braves still maintained their focus towards the Brigantes, making steady yet precarious progress up the slope, but this was futile for King Alfred gave another command shouting, "Loose!"

For the first time in Celtic history, they resorted to what was thought to be the most cowardly of acts and set wave upon wave of arrows through the sky and down on to the defenceless men and women below. No matter how far they ran, they could not escape the skill of the bowmen and once again the survivors fled to the sanctuary of the forest. Another massacre had transpired without the Brigantes having drawn a single sword.

*

The army below was now reduced by half again and returning scouts estimated their numbers to be around two to three thousand, with half of those injured and many more suffering dehydration and hunger. King Alfred, armed with this information, took with him a band of skilled hunters. He had about two hundred men and together they stealthily approached the enemy camp, which was extremely makeshift and unfit for purpose. Alfred waited until the wind was in his favour and ordered his men to set alight the forest that engulfed the enemy camp. Most of the camp was asleep and oblivious to the danger as the King's most stealthy hunters had picked off the many lookouts with their hunting bows.

The flames took hold of the dry forest extremely quickly, killing everyone who was too slow to escape. Any stragglers were quickly finished off with a swift barrage of arrows.

*

King Alfred returned to the fortress, weary from the act of cowardice that his men were forced to show in this battle. He called upon everyone present and spoke in a loud yet solemn manner. "This week, this day and this hour have been marred by wretched acts of war that no clansmen should ever have to face.

I want you to seek comfort from this that the orders were mine, the plans were mine and the burden is mine to the grave. I acted to protect my people in the only way I knew, against a cowardly army that would sneak into battle, unannounced. I want you all to know that the only way to beat these cowards was to resort to cowardly tactics."

The speech was heartfelt and reached the ears of his people, who greeted it with warmth and sympathy as they shouted, "You had no choice. Your guile and cunning have saved our people. Long live the king! Long live the King!")

Chapter 16

The Crossing of the Land of the Lakes and Mountains

Breanna was the last to see it but when it did, it was with reverence for here was a creature older than time that had powers beyond belief. Here was the diamond snake, the adder and she had never seen one before. Breanna went to pick it up and Vaughan scoffed. "Breanna, stop! Beware the kiss of the diamond serpent. Its kiss will kill you stone dead."

Quickly Breanna retreated and the snake slithered into the long grass. King Maccus sighed. "That was close."

Delano was scouting the land in his wolf form, for now they were reaching unknown territory. They were approaching the borders of what they called the high lands, where no man had trod since the ice age. Although the climate was nearly always quite temperate in those days the high lands were still extremely cold in winter. It was as if these lands never regained the warmth that was stolen by the ice age. They were extremely rugged, hence the fact that nobody had ever settled there before. It seemed like madness that the group were trudging ever northwards but that is where the stars were leading them so they followed the stars and followed their hearts.

Tiernon felt eerily comfortable, but with that feeling he also felt vulnerable, as if the silence and tranquillity was on the verge of disturbance. Kael felt it too and he kept himself battle hardened, practicing sword skills daily on his journey. Breanna was ever the hunter, providing the meat for the pottage.

The group made a small camp and settled by a modest fire. Vaughan began roasting the meat with heather and other herbs he had collected on the way. The group sat silently taking in the sheer beauty of the land that surrounded them. Everywhere they looked was a large hill or mountain and numerous lakes dotted about in the distance.

Delano strolled back into camp. "I have good news for Trahern and bad news for the rest of us."

Trahern replied inquisitively, "What is the news?"

Delano continued to explain, "There are vast lakes that hamper our way through this land that we must cross. It is the end of the road for the ponies, we must set them loose."

The group looked slightly sombre yet laughed when Trahern let out a mighty sigh of relief. He simply hated four legged animals.

Tiernon looked towards Delano as he asked, "How far before we reach the first lake?"

Delano replied as he gestured the way. "Three miles or so in that direction. There is a wood just ahead that continues into the hills. We can gather timber to make canoes. They need to be light enough to carry as we have more than one lake to cross."

Breanna quizzed him further, "What if we make buckskin boats, I can dry some out for you?"

Tiernon shook his head as he replied. "Not strong enough, we cannot tell what creatures lurk in these waters. We need a boat with a little rigidity."

*

The group made their way to the wood, and each member took an axe and chopped down a suitable tree, seeking out the best birch.

146

They made a canoe from the bark of the birch tree, which they skilfully stripped and stretched over wooden frames that they made from splitting the logs so thinly as to make ribs that were pliable and light. One suitable piece of wood was used to fashion the paddle. The frames were held together with string made from nettles collected on the journey and the bark was moistened with water to stop it from splitting. Finally, the bark was stitched to the frame with the nettle rope and the holes were glued with bark resin and fire ash to seal them and make the boats watertight yet rigid and light. With their new lightweight canoes held above their heads, the group set out towards the lakes.

When Kael saw the first lake he could not believe his eyes. "This lake is more like the sea. Where does it end?"

Tiernon replied with a grave look, "Not here I hope. I want you all to stick close together in a tight group, no wandering off in front in case we are attacked by some creature of the murk."

*

They pushed their canoes into the water until all seven vessels were afloat, then began paddling across. As they ventured further out they could feel that the lake was very deep. The waters were clear, but a tide rippled through it that unnerved everyone as the canoes bounced from side to side. Kael noticed that the water was very cold as he stroked it with his fingers, making him shudder from shoulder to toe. Vaughan scorned at him. "Keep your hands out of the water."

Every now and again one or all members of the group noticed large, silver ripples in the water that were not the waves. They were made by an animal of some sort; long, lithe and slippery. They were in fact large eels; shoals of them searching for food in waters that contained very little opportunity. The sight of the boats made them curious and they nudged them with the intent to split the pack.

Teirnon grew very nervous, but he said calmly. "Do not let them get between the boats. Keep paddling, steady away."

Delano paddled around Kael. "Keep the children in the centre."

Breanna stuck her chin in the air. "Children indeed."

Steadily, nervously, anxiously, the group crossed the lake until they reached the dry land in safety.

They wandered on across the rugged terrain where the land opened out and the wind bit at their faces. They made camp and waited for night; the way forward was confusing because the sun was highest in the sky and everywhere looked the same. It was time to wait for the stars to appear.

*

That night with the stars in full view, the group followed the North Star towards their fate. After a few hours following the rugged landscape, they noticed another large lake, shimmering in the distance as it reflected the moonlight. The waves were bobbing gently, casting eerie shadows towards the travellers. Each carrying their trusty handmade canoes meant that walking was slow. Vaughan's vessel was the quaintest as he had built it to specification so his was the smallest. The group continued walking in a straight line with their canoes bobbing above their heads. They had inadvertently formed themselves in size order from the smallest to the tallest and if an unseen eye of an owl or fairy spirit could have spied them from above, it would have made them giggle.

As they got nearer the water's edge they lowered their boats gently on to the surf and paddled their way steadily across, keeping a tight formation.

Kael looked about across the lake and said to the group. "This one looks bigger than the other; I can barely see the other side."

Vaughan replied. "This lake seems more intimidating than the other, I do not like it one bit. I think we should keep our wits about us, I think I just spotted an eel."

Delano responded as he scanned the depths with his keen eyes. "There is more than one, there are seven of the beasts circling us, but they are bigger than the others."

King Maccus looked towards Trahern the Bucca. "I know what these creatures are. What do you think Trahern?"

Trahern responded with a tremble in his voice. "There is no mistaking that these creatures must be Peists."

King Maccus retorted. "I knew it. This is not good."

Tiernon then warned the whole group. "It would be wise to remain silent, keep together, keep your eyes and ears open and paddle lightly."

Suddenly his canoe was nudged quite abruptly from behind, splitting him from his comrades. Simultaneously the group found themselves in the same position as the seven deadly Peists each took their turn nudging the group further apart. Kael was the first to be physically attacked when the Peist that was bothering him leapt clean from the water and slid along the front of his canoe, leaning its full weight on it, so that the boat took on water. As the front of the canoe filled up the Peist wriggled back into the murk and Kael had the chance to see its full size. Its head was indeed like that of an eel, except its teeth were many and sharp and its mouth extended the full length of its head. It had bright yellow eyes that were veined with thick blood vessels that added to its macabre appearance. Its girth was very thick and as he watched it slip back into the water he noticed that it was about the size of Delano if not more, so this creature was easily seven or more feet in length.

Instead of panicking, the well-trained warrior boy kept his cool and slowly drew his sword from its scabbard and watched in case the beast boarded the canoe again. The front end of his vessel was now fully submerged but the small boat stayed afloat and Kael edged his way to the back where he caught fleeting glimpses of the silver beast as the moon unveiled it from its hiding places in the deep water. He watched it bob in and out of sight taking mental notes of its former position, as if trying to predict where it would surface next, until suddenly and swiftly once he was sure he was correct Kael sprang into the water with his sword aloft and struck down into the blackness.

He was both swift and accurate and his sword struck the foul creature clean through the skull. The Peist's eyes looked up in their sockets as the beast's life ebbed away and it gave out a death cry that could be heard from across the lake. As its body gave way each morsel of life it shook and quivered, propelling the beast along with Kael, who was still clinging to his sword, deeper into the freezing depths. As soon as chance allowed and the beast was truly dead, Kael withdrew his sword and returned to the surface, swimming frantically towards the shore.

Breanna was as wily as her brother; she too did not panic. She drew her bow and scanned the water for a sight of her pursuer; she heard the eerie screams of the peist that Kael had just killed. She immediately looked in the direction of the scream, luckily for her; just as her head turned, she saw that another peist that obviously wanted to eat her, had leapt clean from the water and was heading straight towards her with its jaws fully open. Had she not turned at that precise moment and had she not seen it in time, it would have surely swallowed her whole. But she did see it and she acted like lightning, letting loose her arrow with full force and skill, hitting the beast clean between the eyes. The arrow killed the beast on contact.

The beast almost hit Breanna as it skimmed across her falling lifeless into the black water. Breanna was skilful enough to avoid contact by lying backwards in the canoe as she let her arrow fly, but it was close, had she not been so swift and skilful she would be in the creature's belly and not in the safety of her vessel. She took a deep breath and let out a huge sigh of relief but suddenly she became aware of loud splashing and once again she drew her bow. She scoured the water in the direction of the noise until she located something squirming frantically in the water making huge ripples on the surface. At first she thought it possible that it was one of the creatures feasting on her comrades but she did not act hastily, instead she drifted closer to get a better look. Good thing for her brother that she chose to be so cautious for it was he whom she was drifting towards and he was desperate to stay afloat in the freezing water. He gurgled as her boat ventured closer and he saw that his sister had her deadly bow in his direction. "Glug, glug, do not shoot. It is me. Help me, I am drowning!"

Breanna threw down her bow and grasped her brother by his cold wet hand. With all her might she pulled him into her boat and he sat trembling violently with the cold.

Breanna asked. "Where is the creature that was pursuing you?"

Kael held his head high in smugness and replied. "Dead, stone dead with one swipe of my sword. Beat that sister."

Breanna, always in competition replied. "Dead with one arrow and I did not lose my boat."

Kael was beaten again by his sister, as always, and he grunted a steam of air from his nose.

Delano was now in the water. The peist that was bothering him had tipped his canoe clean upright with a well-timed blow. Delano transformed into the bear and made himself as big as he possibly could. The peist was quick on the attack and sprang up from the depths below with its mouth wide open. Delano grasped the beast with one hand by the throat and although the girth was thick, he managed to grab a large amount of skin into his hand. With the other he formed a solid fist and cracked the monster hard on the top of its head, sending the beast into a daze. He seized his chance, quickly wrapping his arms around the Piests huge neck and squeezed with all his might until every last breath of air was throttled from the monster. He quickly swam towards little Vaughan who was already in the water. Fortunately for him, the peist thought that he was easy prey and chose to circle him whilst picking at his clothes with its teeth. The beast was playing with its food. Delano swam stealthily closer, Vaughan spotted him in the water and his fear turned to relief, but he did his best not to give the game away. The peist was far too busy relishing the torment and did not even notice the huge black bear that was upon him until it was entirely too late. With one smash of his mighty fist to the back of the creature's head, it was all over. The peist was dead; his brains were crushed by the force of the blow.

Delano gestured to Vaughan, "Climb on my back and I will get you to the other side."

Vaughan hauled himself on to Delano's back and the pair headed for the shoreline at the opposite side of the lake.

Tiernon was whipped from left to right and he held tightly to the sides of his canoe desperate not to fall out, or allow his boat to turn over in the water. He was very successful. The peist tried several times to upturn the boat but Tiernon's balance was remarkable. At last the peist let go of his canoe, perhaps for a breath or perhaps to get a better grip, but it proved to be a huge mistake. As soon as Tiernon was able to let go of the sides of the vessel he held out his hands and shot his massive thunderbolts towards the creature. The water boiled and steam rose from it as the creature's body was blown to small fleshy pieces, which filled the sky like a geyser. Tiernon noticed that his energy was no longer drained from his body when he released his thunderbolts and he could muster much more powerful blows than ever before.

Not sure if any of his comrades had made it, he paddled slowly towards the shore searching the waters as he went.

*

King Maccus almost had his canoe dragged clean to the other side of the shore. With a mighty swoop of his hammer he hit the beast so hard between the eyes that it sank three feet below, before returning to the surface stone dead.

So it was that they all made it to the other side, but Trahern was nowhere to be seen. They searched the land and scanned the water for hours. Delano approached the group after another excursion around the coast. "It is no good, I cannot see him anywhere and if he was unharmed, he would be here by now."

Teirnon looked sad as he replied. "We shall camp here till morning to give him a chance."

So it was decided; the group made camp on the shoreline and lit a small fire, vigilantly waiting for the hopeful return of their friend. Once the camp was settled the group sat round the fire warming themselves, those who had been in the water began steaming as their clothes were drying near the heat. Delano dried for a while but soon felt the urge to turn into the Eagle and without warning he soared into the air and across the lake in search of his friend. Everyone was shocked at his sudden departure and their attentions were fixed upon his silhouette as he sailed back and forth above the lake. They were so intent on him that none of them noticed the small stout figure walking towards them, with a canoe dragging behind him in one hand and the huge bulging body of a peist over his shoulder, until he plopped the creature to the ground in front of them as he spoke. "Anyone fancy a fish for dinner?"

Vaughan laughed loudly as he embraced his friend tightly and the group hugged each other as they jumped about in small circles.

Delano, hearing the commotion, returned to join the group and partook the hugging and the leaping.

Later that night the camp tucked into a lovely meal of peist and herbs. It was really tasty, not half as bad as it looked and very satisfying, especially when it was a meal that had intended to eat them in the first place!

Chapter 17

Shylah gathers the armies

King Alfred, battle weary and full of troubles, was once again summoned by the great Shylah. He approached the water's edge and Shylah rose from beneath the still pool, shimmering with beauty that radiated from her whole being, but she looked increasingly troubled by her thoughts as she spoke to Alfred. "Your troubled mind reaches my thoughts but behold there was no other way. You fought for the good of mankind and that should be appeasement enough. The men and women you killed were on the side of the Evil One."

King Alfred replied in earnest. "I know this my lady, but the feeling still burns in my belly and my heart is heavy. Please tell me, what do you require of me today?"

Shylah looked sternly towards King Alfred and spoke. "Your brave deeds and honour towards this cause are duly noted, you are a good man and your soldiers are well trained. I fear that I have need of you to perform another deed in aid of the quest."

King Alfred was in awe and bowed on bended knee as he asked. "Please tell me what I must do. My sword is yours, my life is yours".

Shylah replied. "I have visions of a great ambush that is awaiting our weary friends as they travel towards their goal. Although my vision does not allow me the insight to view the promised location, I can see the border between two great lands and I can see where there lies a vast natural ridge, where two lands joined as one in an ancient collision. It is close to this ridge that an army of evil men and beasts will meet our friends as they try to cross a large lake. I can see the army gathered at the lake and I can see them rush into the lake, swimming towards the stranded group who are aboard a wooden raft and my vision ends there. I must ask you to muster your best soldiers and take enough supplies to head off this army and halt their attack. You will be fighting in unknown terrain and against an unknown foe."

King Alfred arose as he replied. "I will do this, but I need to know where and when."

Shylah responded. "I can offer you a description of the journey you must take, as I can see the steps that my brother has followed and the steps that he has yet to take in my mind's eye, but they are unclear. You must go in haste and take as many good strong men and animals as you can spare."

King Alfred responded loyally. "Your will be done, my lady."

The pair spoke on for a time and Shylah gave the best directions that her visions would allow. King Alfred carefully drew detailed maps based upon her brief descriptions. They laid careful plans and gave each other heartfelt goodbyes as Shylah disappeared back into the waters that imprisoned her.

*

King Alfred summoned his council and they spent the next two days putting together their best battle strategies and made tough decisions on who to take and who to leave behind. With debate upon debate and plan upon plan, they finally made their decisions and rallied the clans together to give the news.

King Alfred faced his loyal subjects while he spoke in earnest. "It has fallen upon me to gather an army together of my most trusted and loyal soldiers, who will be expected to travel across rough country as fast as your fitness will allow and arrive at your destination in good form and battle ready. It is therefore important for me to pick the best of the best."

King Alfred paced nervously up and down, as he did not want to upset any of his men, for he knew the people left behind would feel highly insulted as all soldiers were born and raised to fight and do their part. To be left out of battle was a smear on their good name. The King spoke on. "I want you all to know that this has been a very difficult and painful decision to make, but the soldiers that I leave behind should feel proud that I leave you in the trusted position of protecting the villagers and their temporary dwellings."

Abruptly a voice broke in from the crowd, rudely because the King was speaking and surprisingly because this was not etiquette. "Excuse me, Sire, but before you insult a single soldier with your choices, could I politely suggest that we all come along?"

King Alfred was taken aback and he questioned. "Take you all?"

The voice replied. "We all took part when leaving our homes to come to this forsaken place. We all took part to escape the fearsome Cythrawl and we all took part to defend Roulston Scar from an army many times our size. The quest that the chosen ones have taken is for all our sakes. Before you give us your decision I feel it only fair to ask the people what they think, as I am sure that all of us, and I speak for all of us, would like the chance to defend the chosen ones in their hour of need."

King Alfred was genuinely touched by this offer and he mulled it over for a moment before responding. "We need to be swift in our travels, we cannot afford to be held back by children and the elderly, we cannot be held back by animals or the sick."

Another voice broke in. "I beg your pardon, sire, but we should not leave anyone behind in case the invaders return. Without the protection of all the soldiers they would surely be in grave danger."

King Alfred looked towards the crowd. "Gather every man, woman, child and animal that wishes to come. We march together."

The crowd erupted in cheers and whistles and the clansmen and women raised their hands in salute, whilst chanting battle cries and indicating their readiness to take arms and journey to the aid of the chosen. They became quite rowdy and the King was touched by their support. He waved his arms aloft to calm the crowd, but the cheering went on for many minutes before the King shouted over the din. "We leave at first light."

The crowd erupted again and a celebration feast broke out with singing and the drinking of beer. The Celts needed little excuse for a good knees up and this was as good as any!.

*

The next morning with sore heads, the crowds met at the gate of the fort with their animals and what little belongings they could muster; they awaited the King's command to go forward. Once outside the fort, the King halted the procession and gave orders for some of his men to burn the fort to the ground. He also ordered his subjects not to look back but only forwards with stout hearts. His strategy was a wise one, as he did not want such a good fort to fall into the wrong hands and he did not want his subjects to lose heart at the sight of all their hard work ending in smoke.

The fort went up in lashes of flames that spread quickly throughout, consuming living quarters and fences alike, warming the backs of the necks of the crowds who were making their way down the steep slope of Roulston Scar, but true to their orders not a single person looked back.

*

Meanwhile Shylah appeared in the waters of the deep cave where Tiernon had defeated Elgon, the swamp dragon. Her appearance was a surprise to the unwary Bucca that was filling his cup with water, but at the same time her arrival was a pleasure as he was captivated by her beauty. Shylah wasted no time with formalities and spoke swiftly. "My name is Shylah, I am the Lady of the Lake and I need to speak urgently with your leader. I have news of your comrade, Trahern."

The Bucca did not need telling twice and responded immediately. "I shall go get the elders, my lady".

He ran off into the murk and disappeared in the darkness. Shylah could hear his little footsteps as he navigated the long dark corridors and was gone.

A few moments later she could hear a great many footsteps heading in her direction and a murmur of many voices buzzing towards her like that of a swarm of busy bees. They came nearer until a large crowd enveloped the pool. One of the Bucca stepped to the front. He rather looked like Trahern but a little younger, not surprising really, as he was Trahern's brother, Eoghan, whose name means young warrior or young wolf, but there was no time for introduction as urgency was in the air.

Shylah recognised his authority and immediately spoke to him. "I have news of your kinsman, Trahern, who travels with the brave ones in their quest for good. I have seen that they will run into a terrible trap and I believe that your help will be needed."

Without a single hesitation Eoghan replied. "Tell me what we must do."

Shylah spoke in the same way she had to King Alfred and spent time going through the same plan with the many Bucca until both parties agreed on what must be done, then without warning she left them, abruptly, as she had other important places to be.

Likewise, Eoghan wasted no time in gathering his people together and they wasted no time in settling on the right plan of action. Even before the day was dawning, a stream of Bucca were pouring out of the safety of their caves, moving unnaturally fast and clad in all manner of battle armour and chain mail, with weapons suited more for digging it would seem than for warfare. Their chosen protections were the mattock and the picks, which were small yet sturdy and hung in their little belts. They were small in stature but very broad in the shoulders and strong in the arms. The army of Bucca swarmed northward in a vast broad formation and it was impossible to count their number.

*

Meanwhile Shylah rose in a shallow pool next to a rather surprised creature that was fishing from a small island in the middle of the pond. "What a specimen I have tempted on my hook. Who might you be?" The creature questioned. Shylah eyed the creature from top to bottom. He had the look of Vaughan but much older and a little more hardened in the features. He looked as if he had seen a battle or two, but Shylah needed to be sure. "My name is Shylah. I am the Lady of the Lake and I am searching for the Hobgoblin named Conrad. Would you be the same creature that I seek?"

The creature threw his fishing line down on to the water and quickly assumed a lowly posture and cowered to his knees in reverence. "The great and beautiful Shylah, it is an honour to grace your presence. I have had the privilege to meet your honourable brother and I have vowed to be of humble service whenever the need arises."

Shylah was glad to hear it, she wasted no time explaining the current situation and Conrad agreed to gather an army of hobgoblin soldiers. With the same careful planning as before Shylah gave the best instructions that she could and left once again in a hurry.

Conrad was up like a shot and ran all the way to his village past the third largest boulder on the right behind the tall grass that grew by the marsh marigold.

He spoke sternly to his men. "Soldiers of the old race, it is once again time to join the humans in battle. We fight not the dark elves as in olden days, but this time we face the Evil One. Our time for honour is upon us and I must ask all able-bodied men to stand with me. Who's with me?"

There was a very slow response with only a small number of volunteers, as older hobgoblins were trying to encourage younger hobgoblins to join arms. Conrad spoke again, this time with a hint of desperation. "We fight for Tiernon the mighty."

Suddenly the atmosphere changed and the crowd shouted loudly in praise of Tiernon and every single male of fighting age put up his hand in volunteering gestures. It was customary in those days that only the males of the species did the fighting. After much deliberation and planning the soldiers left for their destination, travelling by nightfall in great waves with unnatural speed and guile and relative silence, considering their great numbers. They were armed to the teeth with tridents and spears and wore silver chainmail that shimmered like silk. On their belts they wore short swords in scabbards studded with jewels. These were not weapons of their own making, they had stolen them during a raiding of the northern dwarf caves many years ago in the olden days.

*

Shylah rose again in the water in the marshes of the east country, right in front of a pack of thirsty beasts that were busy drinking together by the lake. The sight of so many creatures drinking together at the water's edge was rather eerie as wolves drank next to bears, that drank next to horses and horses drank next to eagles. Eagles drank next to spooky looking creatures with long ears, long limbs and satanic smirks with many teeth in their mouths. Upon the sudden sight of Shylah they bolted out of the water as if they had spied a predator in the depths, but quickly returned when they realised that it was the apparition of a beautiful woman. Shylah wasted no time in speaking. "My name is Shylah and I search the elders of your kind."

"What kind might that be fair lady?" Said the tall gangly creature.

Shylah scowled. "Watch your insolence, Pooka. I know who you are, I know what you are and you should know better. I am the Lady of the Lake and your kind is bound to my brother for all your days."

The creature bit his lip and bowed low. "Forgive me my Lady. It has been many years since I saw you last, my eyes deceived me."

Shylah had no time for idle chat and she asked for a council with the elders immediately. They gathered without question and sat round the lake in a large mass. The elders were at the forefront and the rest sat behind, crossed legged. The entire pack had returned to their usual shape and form, rather human like yet hideous and hairy.

Shylah addressed the group, "I need you to help your lost brother, Delano. He is the most trusted servant and loyal friend to Tiernon the mighty and I fear that they are both in grave danger and need your assistance.

The oldest and most esteemed elder spoke. "How is my son?"

Shylah replied softly, "He is well, yet for how much longer I cannot say. The bold group that he travels with are heading directly towards a large army of humankind and beast kind alike and some stronger power than I care to mention. The Evil One himself has joined the rabble. He blocks my thoughts with his power and will not permit me to contact my brother."

"Does he still travel with the twins?" asked Delano's father.

"He does. His cause is of utmost importance, but as you know Delano is no longer a servant, but he is our most trusted friend," Shylah replied.

"You need not plead anymore. My name is Diablo and I am forever at your service. Simply tell us what we must do?"

So it was, as the times before, that Shylah laid out her story to the pack and made careful plans and gave strict instructions and directions to the listeners.

Once she was sure that they were in unison, she left.

The Pooka then gathered themselves together in a great army and set off on the journey towards the chosen ones. Impressively, they all turned into large eagles and took to the skies in a swirling ball, like a typhoon on a path of destruction swirling around as they soared higher into the sky.

From all corners of Briton armies were on their way north towards the brave heroes, who were heading unwittingly towards death.

Chapter 18

The Battle of the Border

Onwards travelled the courageous team of heroes, through green fields of tall bracken that grew in thickets along the rolling hills and valleys. The band were unaware of the danger that lay ahead, however Tiernon was troubled. He gestured to Delano who instantly joined his side. Tiernon spoke low so as not to arouse any unnecessary suspicion from the group. "I have heard nothing from Shylah for such a long time now. I would not normally let this trouble me, but my chants to summon her at waters' edges have failed several times and I have heard no chant from her."

Delano looked solemnly towards Tiernon as he questioned, "What do you think is the matter?"

Tiernon gave a worried glance as he replied, "I think there is something strange at hand. Some mysterious forces are at work. The Evil One has power that is far reaching."

Delano acknowledged the statement with a nod, "I must agree that there is definitely a feeling that something is awry yet I must confess that I have no idea as to what it could be."

Tiernon eyed the group to make sure no one was paying too much attention to their conversation before speaking again. "I would like you to drop off quietly from the group and scout the area to a perimeter of about a hundred miles. I know it is far and I ask a lot but take as long as you need. I do not know why but I have a feeling that Shylah is trying to warn me of something, but her messages are not reaching me."

Delano agreed and he dropped off quietly whilst the rest of the group travelled together oblivious, and he was gone. Tiernon asked Vaughan to make camp and they settled in for the night and sat around a warm fire. Trahern was singing one of his favourite mining songs and the twins were trying to learn the lines.

> "We mine by day and sleep by night
> We eat by beeswax candlelight
> We take our picks and mattock tools
> And dig the earth like weary fools
> For gold and tin and silver stones
> In cold damp caves that chill our bones
> Our life is rough and toil is hard
> And that is why we sing this bard."

The song was short and repetitive, but the beat was good and the twins soon got the gist of it. King Maccus found himself humming along and Vaughan was bobbing up and down whilst serving out his freshly cooked hare and fennel stew.

Tiernon gazed up at the night sky with all sorts of unanswered questions whirling around inside his head. Breanna, who never missed a thing, noticed his worried scowl and asked, "What is it that troubles you?"

Tiernon tried desperately to feign a smile but he was not very convincing.

"Nothing dear, I am quite fine" he replied.

Breanna shook her head in disagreement as she asked again. "You do not look fine. I can always tell when you are troubled by your expression."

Tiernon scoffed. "It is nothing to concern you, child."

Vaughan was about to hand Tiernon his food and queried as he passed him the hot bowl. "Beg your pardon master, but I see it too. Something troubles you. Please share your problems. We may be able to help."

Tiernon was never any good at telling lies so he asked the group to gather as he spoke earnestly. "I have had an ill feeling for the last few days, something niggling at me like a bad itch. When I get these feelings I am seldom wrong. Something is not quite right so I have asked Delano to have a sniff about."

King Maccus slurped at his stew as he asked inquisitively. "What do you think is the matter?"

Tiernon tucked into his hearty meal as he replied. "That's just it. I cannot put my finger on it but something is not right. I have had no contact with Shylah and that is what is bothering me so much."

Trahern looked up from his bowl and asked what they should do.

Tiernon thought about his answer whilst chewing a juicy piece of hare and then replied, "Nothing at all for the time being, just hold up here until Delano returns, for I fear to go further."

The group agreed and returned to their eating but this time there was an uneasy atmosphere. Everyone was now wondering whether Tiernon's intuition was correct or not. It usually was.

*

They stayed in camp for two full weeks, keeping busy on small hunting trips and general camp maintenance. Delano was gone for a long time and it became a worry.

The group tried their best to stay busy; Vaughan was passing his time by fishing in a small stream nearby. He was using a homemade fishing line and a fat worm as bait on the end of a slender bone taken from a wild pig that he had cooked up a few days before. He was concentrating hard and was sure he was about to get a bite as his line was being tugged very gently as if tested by some hungry fish below the surface.

As he peered into the water a huge, black shadow crossed his view. At first glance he thought that he had seen a huge fish under the water, but he soon realised that it was a reflection in the lake. He looked up to see the familiar wings of Delano flying high above. He threw his makeshift fishing line into the water and ran to camp shouting. "Delano is back safe and sound everybody, come and see."

Instantly, the group stopped what they were doing and gathered round the campfire, eagerly waiting for Delano to land.

Once back on earth, Delano returned to his true form and his face spoke a thousand words. He looked very grim indeed and rather serious as he spoke.

"There is a huge army gathered about eighty miles from here marching with the speed of the wind consisting of man, beast and other creatures striving together."

King Maccus kicked a stone into the fire as he quizzed. "Do you think they are looking for us?"

Delano nodded with a sad look.

"Most definitely. They are armed to the hilt and determined. I would not like to guess at how many there are because the mass of soldiers seemed endless. They have some evil power on their side as their speed of foot is unnatural. I fear that they may be only four days away."

Tiernon rubbed his chin thoughtfully as he joined the conversation. "We need a plan. We must somehow try to avert them."

Kael scraped at the ground with a dead twig as he quickly asked. "What do you think we should do? Tell me before I burst."

Vaughan wagged his finger in Kael's face as he jumped in. "Let him speak, master."

Tiernon thought for a second, trying to find the best response but there was no good way to say it so he just let it out.

"I fear that the Evil One must be among them. That is why I am unable to contact Shylah because his power must be close by. He must have united evil men and beasts and he must sense my very presence."

Breanna was agitated and a little afraid as she scoffed. "You should have informed us a lot sooner."

Tiernon gave her a woeful look as he replied solemnly, "It was foolish of me. I did not wish to worry anyone, but I have a plan. The Evil One is tracking me. He can feel my presence in the same way I can feel Shylah's. We must split up. I will take King Maccus and Vaughan and head east before tracking north. The rest of you head far to the west before tracking north. That way the danger will lead to me, leaving the chosen ones enough time to sneak into the Northern highlands."

Trahern looked worried for Tiernon and asked. "What about your safety?"

Tiernon waved his hands in dismay, "My safety means nothing compared to the task. It is my destiny to see this to the end. If the end is nearby, so be it."

Kael kicked a stone in the air as he scuffed. "I will miss Vaughan's cooking."

The group laughed heartily for the first time in a long while.

They journeyed about fifty paces from each other, all musing over whether they may ever meet again or who may live or die, when the sun suddenly disappeared amongst a thick blackness and almost all the light faded. Long shadows were cast upon the ground as many beasts circled in the air. Vaughan ran for cover, hiding under a bracken shrub and King Maccus threw himself between two boulders with his hammer tightly gripped for action. The twins crouched together, sword and bow at the ready. Tiernon sighed deeply as if mustering all his might to create his devastating lightning bolts. Delano changed into the wolf, snarling fiercely towards the sky and Trahern flexed his muscles ready to fight to the death. The two groups quickly re-joined each other for safety in numbers as the mass of beasts circled above.

It was hard to tell what the beasts were from the ground as they circled to and fro, seemingly waiting for the best moment to attack. Delano could tell that they looked like some sort of huge flying bird. In fact, they looked like huge black birds. Huge black eagles to be precise. He squinted his eyes to get a better look at the dark swirling mass and locked his sight on one member of the beastly group above. Instantly, Delano howled with delight and returned to Pooka form, waving his arms in excitement, to the bemusement of the rest of the heroes.

"Father," he shouted. "Oh, my father you have come to my aid."

The group eyed each other in speechless awe as one by one huge eagles grounded, turning instantly into creatures they all recognised, the wonderful Pooka.

The stream of eagles landing seemed almost endless and it took an age for every creature to descend safely. Once they were all assembled on the ground there was a mad scramble from everyone alike to welcome and embrace each other.

Delano held his father tightly with eyes filled to the brim. "My father, you came for me. I am forever in your debt."

171

"It has been too long. You keep him all to yourself Tiernon the mighty, it is unfair of you!" giggled Diablo.

Tiernon instantly recognised a very old and dear friend and said warmly. "Diablo, it truly has been far too long."

The Pooka were too numerous to count and therefore it was hard for everyone to speak, so they split into groups and began talking amongst themselves. They had brought provisions and tools with them in cloth sacks carried in their talons and were busily unpacking them and sorting out food parcels and rummaging through the tools.

Diablo informed Tiernon and his comrades about the message from Shylah. Fortunately, she had the wisdom to inform Diablo of the coming of the Bucca and the coming of the hobgoblins and the coming of King Alfred and the entire Northern Brigantes. The twins were delighted. Trahern was also joyous, but mostly Vaughan. Distance and time meant nothing to the long-lived hobgoblin. He was always close at heart to his kin and it seemed so long since he had last seen them. He forgot his worries and danced and skipped, to the amusement of the Pooka.

The most esteemed of the group then gathered in council and discussed tactics. They plotted and schemed through the night, working out from the limited information they had, how long they thought it would take the evil army to reach them. How far away Conrad and the hobgoblins were. How far Eoghan and the Bucca were. How far King Alfred and the Brigantes were. They worked out roughly in days when each band set off and roughly whereabouts they would be. It was a long affair with many interruptions and much drawing on stones and squabbles about who was right or who was wrong. But eventually, as always, Tiernon the mighty had the last word and he made plans to send out Pooka as eagles to search out the saviours that were behind them, giving word and laying plans for a battle.

After long hours of consideration, everyone eventually bedded down for the night in relative safety in numbers. The twins slept the soundest, surrounded by huge Pooka that would wake if a frog farted.

*

The next day three eagles set out in search of the Bucca, hobgoblins and the Brigantes. Meanwhile the Pooka split into distinct groups. Some remained in Pooka form whilst others transformed into horses. Some turned to bears and others scoured the skies as eagles, ready to bring news of anyone approaching. They journeyed easterly, searching for better ground that would favour them more as their current location gave sway to the approaching army. They searched for two days and settled on high ground with a view for many miles. At the top of the huge hillside they could see from their vantage point, a natural curving mountainous ridge that circled out from the hillside, south to north. The ridge resembled the shape of an ancient hoof print, stamped deep into the landscape with many humps and tussocks to hide behind. Trees were present but sparse due to the high altitude, leaving an almost unhindered view for miles around. There was a natural ridge beyond a large lake, deep in the basin to the north that tracked the land from east to west as far as the eye could see. It was a natural landmark that was formed when the earth had once crashed together whilst the universe was still young. It was the exact place where Shylah had prophesied the battle to be.

The camp settled on the hillside in relative safety, keeping vigilant watch whilst they awaited the arrival of the three eagles, musing over the battle to come. The days prior had been trying times for Tiernon, but he was calm now that he had a plan in place. Tiernon liked plans, he hated uncertainties.

*

The first eagle dropped into camp with news of the hobgoblins who were but half a day away and then later the second eagle came with news of the Bucca who were only one day away. The third eagle came with news of the Brigantes who had made a truly courageous effort and were only two days away, fully armoured on ponies with carts and laden with supplies.

Tiernon was now at ease and began to think more clearly. He studied in detail the huge lake at the bottom of the valley. He noticed that the natural ridge that stood north of the lake gave way to a rolling valley that funnelled towards the lake, where a natural glacier had once rolled down the land to where the lake now sat. He realised that this would act as a natural trap, where the enemy would hopefully follow the landscape towards the lake. He sent some Pooka bears down to scout around and report back its estimated width and depth. Armed with this information Tiernon had a great idea and he sent Delano in eagle form to fly southwards as fast as his wings could take him to summon Shylah in a lake far away from the power of the Evil One. Delano burst into flight, keeping track of all the natural landmarks in his brilliant memory.

*

That evening the hobgoblin army strolled into camp to the joy of everyone. After many hugs they were quickly put to work by Tiernon, who ordered some of them to make a raft from the available wood in the area. He ordered that the hobgoblins make crude, wooden cut outs in the likeness of the travelling comrades Breanna, Kael, Trahern, King Maccus and Vaughan.

The rough, wooden cut outs were made to specification resembling the real people and they were crudely tied to the makeshift raft.

This was carried to the bottom of the steep hillside and put to rest on the beach by the huge lake.

Tiernon was by the lake overlooking the proceedings when he sensed the presence of his sister, Shylah. Delano had successfully summoned her and gave her the location of her brother. She appeared in full battle clothing, astride her huge battle ox and of course with Excalibur and scabbard on her person; but not for herself because her plan was for Tiernon to wield the great sword, safe in the knowledge that no harm could come to him while he wore the scabbard of Excalibur. No foe could beat the army of the leader who held the great sword.

Tiernon gave Shylah his trusty Celtic sword in exchange for Excalibur and it fit him perfectly.

"What do you think?" he asked his sister.

"It looks much better on me, old one." she replied, referring to his white hair.

He gave her a stern, yet loving glance followed by a smile. "You know what you must do. We need to draw out their first contingent and test their strength."

"I know what I must do. Take care brother," and she was gone beneath the depths with her trusty battle ox.

Tiernon had no time to ask of Delano, but he surmised that Shylah travelled in the blink of an eye so it would take Delano another day to return. Everything was falling nicely into place as if the power and might of the Creator was with Tiernon that day.

*

Tiernon cast a spell on the craft that carried his wooden comrades and sent the raft drifting to the centre of the huge lake. Through his magic he caused it to halt on the spot and then an anchor stone, tied to a long rope, fell by the power of Tiernon's mind into the depths. He sat in meditation until suddenly a doppelganger of himself appeared on the boat and waved towards him from the raft. Tiernon waved back at himself and chuckled because this was one of the favourite tricks that he had learnt as a young Druid boy and it never failed to work.

Tiernon then joined the rest of his hidden army of hobgoblins and Pooka in the hills behind the large semi-circular ridge and his doppelganger on the raft sat patiently waiting.

*

The next morning Delano returned from his venture and flew past the raft with a nod to let Tiernon know that everything was in place. Tiernon on the raft waved in conformation. Delano then landed at the other side of the large hill and took his place with the rest of the huge army. He gave a startled look as Tiernon approached him, to which Tiernon just chuckled and said. "I will explain it to you later."

A portion of the Pooka horses set off southward to meet King Alfred to lend their backs. They formed a huge cavalry and headed towards the waiting heroes. The Bucca were just appearing over the brow of the hill. They had been intercepted by scouting Pooka and were approaching stealthily towards the south side of the hills. The hobgoblins had scouted the lands southwards for their old friends, the grey wolves. They had convinced the wolves to carry them on their backs, forming a cavalry hidden quietly behind the huge hill on the south side, where Tiernon and his comrades were camped. Some hobgoblins preferred to stay on foot and go into battle the old way. The Pooka bears hid in the hills further east, where the mountainous scar gave way to the rolling hills that led to the valley below. The Pooka eagles hid all around in the hills and mountains, waiting with eyes peeled sharply into the distance. Tiernon's doppelganger waited patiently alongside his wooden friends in the centre of the lake.

*

The approaching army of evil menace approached their goal. Evil powers quickened their pace and sharpened their wits. They had travelled a monumental distance, originally making their way from the far south and marching the entire length of the country. These legions were gathered by the Evil One after the battle of Roulston Scar, following the news regarding the total defeat from the Brigantes tribe.

The Evil One was unaware that Tiernon had worked out a cunning plan and that his army of men, goblins, dwarves and the menacing Bwgond race of shape shifters were heading into a trap. The Bwgond had taken the guise of wolves and allowed a great portion of goblins to ride upon their backs, but their evil ran deep so they resembled the wolf in stature and shape, but were a grim, earthy charcoal colour with huge bat like ears and menacing yellow eyes. They had teeth as sharp as spears inside huge gaping jaws. Their legs were long and gangly with huge paws full of thick, sharp claws. The Bwgond truly was a foe to be utterly feared, for they could shape shift at will into almost any animal guise that they wished, yet their evil appearance always gave them away. The army was traveling with great speed and a great rumbling could be heard far and wide as they thundered onwards like a rolling earthquake.

*

They were soon within sight of Tiernon, the doppelganger, who sat waiting steely eyed in his small makeshift raft, surrounded by his wooden cut out friends. Anything that the doppelganger saw, Tiernon could also see from his safe hiding place. Anything that his doppelganger heard, Tiernon heard from his hiding place. Tiernon spotted the oncoming foe. The sheer sight made his heart leap from his chest as he wondered if the hobgoblins, Bucca, Pooka and men would be enough to fend off such a huge army.

*

The land disappeared under the dark swirl of monsters that were approaching fast. They raced through the natural funnel towards the great lake and upon seeing the craft floating gently in the middle of the great lake, slowed their pace until they moved in unison like a stalking wolf.

At the water's edge, the first to arrive came to a standstill as their eyes deceived them; they spied Tiernon and his comrades like sitting ducks upon the surface of the lake. The goblins and Bwgond had keen eyesight and had it not been for the trickery and magic of Tiernon's secret chanting, the game would have been over in an instant because the beasts would have realised that the crew was made of timber.

Tiernon bewitched them with his chanting and their eyes deceived them. A great roar of laughter filled the air and the Evil One made his way through the large mass of men and beasts.

Tiernon looked in awe through the eyes of his doppelganger as the Evil One ventured closer to the shore. He seemed to glide rather than walk and his size was great due to the power that he had gained through the failings of men.

The Evil One was tall yet slender and was adorned in a material that resembled thick leather armour. A long, black robe hung from his shoulders and a black head guard hid his face from view.

The clothes were forged from iron created deep in the underworld where the evil power gave the material great strength, yet a mystical suppleness and lightness, giving the appearance of a flexible material. The Evil One had come a long way since the days of crawling on his belly as a serpent.

He spoke to Tiernon with his mind as the craft was too far from the shore to hear spoken words.

"I have waited an age to see the end of your kind, mighty Tiernon. You have been a curse to my cause since the day you were born. I just wish you had made things a little harder for me and a little more sporting."

Tiernon could hear what his doppelgänger's mind could hear, but he had to be careful and speak through the doppelganger's mind and not his own. He replied defiantly, "You are still a great worm. Even though you now stand upon two feet, you spend your immortal life slithering for the pickings of man. You are but a leech that sucks dry the hopes of mankind. Send your many men and beasts into the lake and watch my small band of men defeat all that enter. We fight of our own free will and not because we are trapped by words and weighed down by greed and lies."

This was an enormous insult that the Evil One could not bear and it sent him into a rage, which is exactly what Tiernon was hoping for. Without any rational thought, the Evil One sounded the attack and every available man, beast or goblin upon the hideous Bwgond dived straight into the lake and swam towards the stricken raft. The lake was alive with men and beasts, all wanting to be the first to get a taste of flesh and gain their reward for bringing the heads of the chosen ones back to shore.

All the while the doppelganger of Tiernon mocked defiantly. "You will see, you will see that you can't kill me."

This mocking infuriated the men and beasts and they swam faster towards the raft until they were within feet of their helpless victims.

Other men and beasts were still entering the lake. So huge was their fury that the masses dived in the lake to get a piece of Tiernon and his crew, who seemed to mock them without a care in the world. The real Tiernon remained hidden with his army behind the great hill, quietly chanting his magical spell, deceiving all comers into believing that his wooden comrades were alive and moving about the raft hurling insults left and right.

*

The enemy was so close that they could almost touch the raft, and still they could see Tiernon and his friends laughing in the face of death. The lake was literally bursting with bodies. So powerful was Tiernon's magic that the entire mass of men and beasts swimming towards the raft became so enraged that common sense was all but gone.

Finally, a goblin that sat upon the back of a large Bwgond grabbed Tiernon the doppelganger by his Belt. At that moment the real Tiernon in his safe hiding place lifted his spell and the surprised army could suddenly see through the deception. The doppelganger disappeared in a puff of smoke and the crew stopped all their chanting and froze like wooden statues.

The surprised goblin fell from his mount, taking in huge gulps of water until he sank to the bottom and drowned.

Tiernon used the power of his mind and spoke to the Evil One, who just stood in shock upon the shore, watching in horror with the realisation that he had been tricked. "If you think that was a clever trick, watch this."

At that moment huge bubbles began to rise in the water and burn the swimmers on the surface. At first the water became just a little uncomfortable, but within a few moments all the water was bubbling furiously like a hot spring on a cool day. All the men and beasts in the water let out huge screams and tried frantically to ignore the pain of what was now scalding, boiling water. Screams and wails of huge magnitude rang out from the lake for several minutes while every creature within was burnt beyond recognition, until everything and everyone in that lake was dead. As bodies sank and floated with the skin peeling off their bones, not a sound could be heard. The silence was deafening and the vast army on the shore looked in sheer terror. Some thought of running as this powerful magic scared them to their souls, but they stood in horror because they were bound by their fear of the Evil One.

The Evil One stood in shock, trying frantically to work out what had just transpired. He could not even fathom a guess at what magic was afoot and he too was in awe of the power that he had just witnessed. He pondered silently until he was put out of his misery when Shylah surfaced on her trusty battle ox, which was still steaming at the nose. The battle ox had boiled the water as it did in the battle against the Grindylow, but the magnitude and the heat was too much for one battle ox. One by one, the heads of steaming battle oxen surfaced to the gasps of their audience on the shore. The lake became full of them, all steaming from their efforts, all without riders except the leader that Shylah was astride. The army looked on bewildered. Shylah steered her ox towards the shore, close by to where the Evil One stood and said in a defiant manner. "Come in if you dare. The water is fine. This is my domain, you snake and this is my army. Enter at your peril, for I am waiting."

She did not give the Evil One any time at all to reply. She sank to the bottom and her army of oxen went with her.

Not a soul wished to step even a toe into the water. They just stared at each other, bewildered and afraid.

The Evil One was furious as he could feel the presence of Tiernon in the hills to the south, now that his clever magic had been lifted and he ordered his men to charge towards the hills, still believing that Tiernon was alone with his small band of friends.

*

During the distraction of the loud skirmish in the lake, the Pooka bears had sneaked down the valley on the east side and the Bucca had sneaked down the hills on the western side, awaiting their chance to join the fray.

Tiernon rose from his hiding place and gave the command for the Pooka and Bucca to attack.

A wave of Pooka eagles led by Diablo launched their onslaught from every direction, hauling the Bwgond wolves from the ground along with their goblin mounts, firing them hard towards other evil riders, using them as ammunition. The Pooka eagles did not have it all their own way however, the goblins were accurate with their spears and took out some numbers with distant throws from deeper within the ranks. A portion of the Bwgond wolves transformed into hideous, grey eagles and took the battle to the skies, ganging up on the Pooka eagles two to one, ripping them apart with their powerful talons.

Pooka eagles were proficient at aerial acrobatics and soon outmanoeuvred the lumbering Bwgond eagles, turning on them swiftly, forcing them into the mountainside with their talons. Although lives were lost on both sides, it was not long before the skies were truly in the hands of the Pooka.

Tiernon arose once again from the safety of the southern hillside and ordered another attack. The Pooka horses, with heavily armed Bucca on their backs, hurtled down the hillside on the far west and the Pooka bears from the east hurtled down the valley.

The two massive parties crashed into the trapped army by the lake and a massive bloody battle ensued. The Bucca raged into battle led by Eoghan and with the advantage of the huge Pooka horses, they trampled all in their path, finishing their helpless foes with blows from their mattocks and picks. They showed no mercy and squashed men, goblins and Bwgonds alike. The mighty Pooka bears did likewise. They needed no weapons as they were armed with claws and sharp teeth, which they used effectively, mauling to pieces every living creature that crossed their path. The two sides worked their way viciously towards the centre of the killing zone; hacking, biting, stabbing and trampling their way to victory until the lakeside was taken.

*

The Evil One retreated from danger as soon as the attack began, protected by his minions. He made his way northwards through the natural valley and led his army towards the land ridge. They circled the horseshoe on both sides, hoping to come back down the south hill to gain the high ground, but Tiernon who was well versed in the arts of battle, had strategized this and he was already circling the western ridge to cut them off, along with a large party of hobgoblins on wolf and foot.

He had ordered another contingent of hobgoblins and wolves, led by Conrad, to cut them off on the eastern side. The Pooka and Bucca had annihilated the armies trapped by the lake and proceeded to chase the enemy northwards up the funnelled valley continuing to fight along the way.

Headed off on both the eastern and western side, both armies clashed in battle. The grey wolves snarled and attacked their foe whilst the hobgoblin riders stabbed with deadly accuracy with their spears and tridents. They received many bites and stabs to their silver chainmail, but no harm bestowed them as the mail had been forged by the dark elves of yesteryear and held special powers. What the hobgoblins lacked in stature they made up for in courage.

*

Tiernon leapt into battle, drawing Excalibur from his scabbard with a loud metallic ring filling the air. The enemy paused for a moment, contemplating whether to flee. Excalibur froze the hearts of the enemy, for its success in battle was renowned. With swift action Tiernon swished and slashed Excalibur left and right, killing everything that got in his way. The sword had a will of its own, blocking all comers from all direction. Excalibur hauled the mighty Tiernon forward in battle. All he could do was hold tight to the sword and follow its will.

King Maccus was close behind him, smashing heads with his mighty hammer, wielding his weapon as if it was as light as a feather. A Bwgond hissed towards him and he smashed it first in the foot then swiftly to the side of the head, sending the rider reeling to the ground. Vaughan grabbed the reeling goblin by the throat and skewered him with his knife. Breanna drew her bow and sent arrows flying towards the enemy, drawing one after the other with speed and accuracy. Kael swished and slashed his way through the fray with his trusty Celtic sword.

The twins fought with great honour and bravery; their childhood innocence was far behind them. Trahern and Delano raged into battle alongside the twins, giving protection from enemy onslaught. Trahern picked up Bwgond wolves single handed, smashing them in the skull as he pulled the goblins limb from limb. The true strength of a Bucca was on display this day.

Delano fought closely by the side of the chosen ones, slashing at all who came within their proximity, inflicting massive damage with his devastating claws and teeth. He transformed constantly from Pooka to Wolf and then to bear when the need arose, smashing every goblin, man and Bwgond that got too close to the twins.

The enemy was now on the run, having been forced northward from both sides. The great mass was fleeing towards the land ridge. If they could make it there in time they could gain the high ground and escape the onslaught.

The battle raged northwards and Tiernon felt heavy of heart as he saw the enemy slip ever closer to escaping the valley's grip. It was at that moment that he heard the battle horn of the Brigantes and then caught sight of a large army of Brigantians on Pooka horseback, led by Alfred, who were clad in iron finery with swords and weapons. They charged over the ridge and down into the valley, trapping the enemy from escape. They trampled their way forwards, slashing and spearing anything that looked ugly.

*

The battle raged on for hours and the enemy formed a huge central ball that protected the Evil One. Tiernon's army picked at the swirl, killing every living creature that dared to fight and the great mass shrank in size, smaller and smaller until the Evil One was in Tiernon's sight. Excalibur sprang into action with a will of its own, striking a blow towards the Evil Lord. With unearthly reflexes, the Dark Lord drew his sword from his scabbard and halted the blows of Excalibur. The two were locked in battle, grabbing and swishing at one another in bitter fury. Every strike was blocked by the great Excalibur as the battle raged on.

Tiernon managed a blow to the arm of the Evil One, who howled like a wolf as the pain surged through him. The Evil Lord drew power from his anger and managed with swift action to grab Tiernon by the shoulders. He pressed his claws deep into Tiernon's flesh and his evil poison coursed through Tiernon's veins. Breanna was quick with her bow. She let fly an arrow that entered the head guard of the Evil One. Kael struck a blow to his leg and King Maccus gave a loud crack to the side of his head with his huge hammer. The Evil One sank to the ground and King Maccus rained a flurry of blows to the chest of the Evil One, crushing the armour with every strike until there was nothing left but a crumpled heap of iron. The Evil One groaned with an unearthly wailing as he disappeared in a cloud of black smoke, which left the battlefield like a whirling tornado.

Tiernon lay stricken. His veins turned black and his eyes turned yellow as he struggled for his life. Every breath sounded like his last and Delano beckoned one of his Pooka comrades to carry Tiernon from the battlefield. The Pooka turned to an eagle and carried Tiernon far away as he held tight to Excalibur.

*

The battle raged for a time until every last creature of evil was crushed into the dust. When the final foe was squashed, the Celts and their comrades cheered loudly and rejoiced, hugging each other as they celebrated their finest victory.

Chapter 19

The Search for the
White Bear Talisman

The fields were a mass of destruction and despair. People were busy collecting their comrades and caring for the sick and dying. Any living man or beast on the side of evil was quickly dispatched and placed on the many piles ready for burning. The hobgoblins suffered very few casualties, which was surprising due to their stature. They were protected by their precious chain mail. They thanked the wolves profoundly and released them back into the wild. The wolves had lost many lives because they fought so bravely.

Conrad was especially pleased with Vaughan. He gave him an admiring smile as he said to him, "You will make a fine warrior one day, master Vaughan."

Trahern found his beloved brother, Eoghan, and gave him a huge bear hug. They worked together collecting the injured and dead comrades to give them treatment and proper burials.

Delano embraced his father, Diablo and together they scoured the battlefield to retrieve the many Pooka that had lost their lives to the cause.

King Maccus shook the arm of King Alfred, "It was an honour to fight alongside your clan. Ours and yours will remain friends always."

They had lost considerable numbers. Although brave in battle, humans were the weakest species. Breanna and Kael sat by the great lake hugging and sobbing. They were devastated at the loss of their beloved protector and father figure, Tiernon. Their sorrow was uncontrollable. They were startled by a voice that called out from the water. It was Shylah, "Why do you weep?"

Breanna sobbed, "Tiernon was killed on the field."

Shylah laughed, to the annoyance of Kael, and he raged out. "How can you laugh at a time like this, and Tiernon, your brother? You should be ashamed."

Breanna pulled him down by the arm fearing his insolence as Shylah replied softly, "I will allow you your disobedience due to your sorrowful situation, but be warned, never speak to me in that manner again."

Kael showed some remorse as he retorted, "I am sorry my lady. I just do not understand how you can be so calm. Tiernon was your brother."

Shylah laughed again. "And he still is."

The twins were bemused so Shylah explained carefully, "Tiernon wielded Excalibur into battle. Excalibur brings victory for all who wield her. He also had on his presence the great scabbard of Excalibur with special powers of its own. Any person who wears the scabbard of Excalibur can sustain no permanent injury. Excalibur's scabbard has the power of healing. Remember the legend; those who wield the scabbard will receive no wound."

Breanna leapt up with joy, "You mean he is still living."

Shylah smiled warmly. "Very much alive and very much healed, carried off the field so that he would not lose Excalibur to the enemy, otherwise things could have been very different. The evil poison was not a match for the great scabbard of Excalibur.

Tiernon waits for you. He is in the Brigantes camp two miles south of here. Go to him."

With new found vigour they ran in search of Delano. Finding him with his father, they helped with the sick and dying. The battlefield took an age to clear and darkness fell as the piles of the evil dead were set ablaze. The flames rose high into the sky casting sinister shadows on the ground and the evil bodies within hissed and spat as they burned to charcoal. A great groaning came from the fires as if the souls of the dead were returning to the underworld and an evil wind howled through the valley, chilling the spines of everyone who stood witness.

*

The next day Kael and Breanna sought council with Tiernon at his bedside. He was fully healed but taking rest and recuperation from his ordeal. The end was in sight at last. A fear had been lifted and a great oppressive weight had been removed from all.

In the days that followed Tiernon gathered all the leaders and spoke to them, "I thank you all from the bottom of my heart. You have truly turned the tides in our favour and I shall be forever grateful for your courage and bravery."

The group of leaders cheered loudly as Delano looked towards his master and smiled. "You are most welcome old friend."

*

The leaders spoke for many hours. Not of strategy but of friendships and alliances, both old and new, between man and beast alike. The great battle had united beasts and man in a friendship that would become timeless.

In the knowledge that they would have to leave each other soon a great party ensued with much drinking and celebration, as was always the case with the Celts. It continued for three whole days. Singing and cheering, drinking and dancing. Eventually, the groups and comrades said their heartfelt goodbyes and drifted away over the coming days.

King Alfred returned to his southern Atrebates Clan and re-joined his son. He returned to a hero's welcome and songs were sung in his name.

The Bucca, hobgoblins and Pooka said their fond farewells and embarked on the long journey back to their homelands.

*

Together, the seven heroes and the Clans of the Brigantes set off north, over the ridgeline border and into the highlands across terrain that they had never seen before.

They crossed huge valleys, dappled on either side with great mountainous hills, travelling for miles and journeying for days on end. They crossed dense forests where the pine trees grew tall and thick. Great herds of deer roamed free pursued only by the grey wolves.

Eagles soared across the open skies, buzzards and kestrels as well as harriers and hawks. This terrain was alive with nature.

The traveling was tough, but food and water were bountiful along the way. As the large group headed northwards, they remained in high spirits. They crossed vast lakes in handmade vessels and climbed large mountains that stood in their way, then traversed deep ravines that blocked their path. Scouring vast forests and plains on their endless quest towards the North, they used the stars by night and skills by day.

*

The group followed a large river that ran towards the sea and skirted in and out around the coast. Tiernon had a feeling about this river and followed it along with his men for days. He peered into the distance and spotted a huge mountainous range to the west, the size of which he had never seen before. He pointed to the group and said loudly, "We must head for those mountains. I feel it. Make camp and we will head there tomorrow."

The group set up a makeshift camp and Tiernon gave orders that the seven heroes make the rest of the journey alone.

*

The next morning Delano woke the twins and gathered the group of seven for the trek towards the mountain range. Leaving the clan behind they said their goodbyes and hastened towards their final goal. Travel was hard and the terrain was unforgiving, but by late evening they closed in on the mountain range and over the next hill brow. As they got closer to the summit the glorious mountain showed itself and Tiernon whispered. "Beinn neamh bhathais." This meant the mountain with his head in the clouds.

Kael gave a puzzled glance toward the mountain top as he asked Tiernon, "What is the white grass that grows on top?"

Tiernon laughed loudly as he replied, "That is not grass my boy. That is snow."

Breanna and Kael stared in wonder as the group continued towards the three mountains, which grew in stature with every step. They looked in awe as they wrapped up in wool skins and warm clothing before they began the long ascent up the sloping hillside. As they reached the summit of the first range they came to an undulation which revealed in full glory the mountain that Tiernon called the mountain with his head in the clouds. They travelled along a thin gully and traversed steep crags until reaching a level track that was hidden under thick snow. They could feel large boulders under their feet. From their vantage point, they could see a large basin where the mountain had once collapsed in on itself a long time ago. Suddenly, the twins stopped as if possessed by some hidden power and spoke in unison. "We dig here. This is the very spot, our destiny is upon us."

Delano cheered with joy, "We have made it at last, we are here."

Vaughn looked positively vexed as he complained. "We are here master. What's good about that? All I see is snow."

Trahern slapped him on the back as he scoffed. "Then we dig, you fool."

The Bucca did what he did best and what he was born to do. He dug with all his might, clearing a large patch of snow and boulders until he revealed the hard rock beneath. He tapped on the hard granite and listened to the sound.

"Nothing here," and tapped again. "No, nothing here either."

The group stood by whilst Trahern tapped and mumbled to himself for a while until very calmly he spoke as he placed the tip of his mattock on to the stone below.

"King Maccus. Would you kindly give this a thump with your great hammer?" He gestured. "I have located a gem within this rock that is unknown to me, but the sound is distinctive."

King Maccus gave the stone a huge whack with his hammer and the granite gave a loud clatter as a small crack appeared.

Trahern adjusted his mattock and said. "Again, King Maccus. Again."

Once again King Maccus swung down his hammer and the crack widened to the sound of a loud chinking of stone.

"Again!" The group yelled with excitement.

King Maccus drew on all is strength and with a mighty swoop his hammer dealt a blow of defiance on the hard rock as it split in two with a huge groan and a crash.

Trahern fell down the gaping chasm that had just appeared before him, almost landing on his face. He scrambled about to find his feet and placed his hands on to what felt like a smooth, wooden box, which he quickly opened to reveal the contents inside. Once he held the treasure firmly in his hand, he discarded the box and shouted up to the onlookers. "I have found something."

Kael replied excitedly, "Throw it to me."

Trahern threw the object towards Kael, who inspected it with great care.

It was a white and shiny disc that was highly polished and made from pure bone, with the image of the White Bear carved neatly into the surface. This was no ordinary piece of jewellery. It was fashioned by the hands of the Gods, long since departed from this world. It was the Talisman of the White Bear, the symbol of the promised land for the clan that would never see defeat.

Kael held it high in the air and cheered loudly.

Tiernon pulled out a rather worn and bedraggled rag from within his clothing. It was the banner made by the hands of Queen Pictania. He took the White Bear Talisman and wrapped it carefully within the banner before handing it back to Kael.

And so it was that the quest was complete. They had discovered the promised land and the tale of the search for the White Bear Talisman was at an end.

*

Tiernon went on to keep his promise to search the bowels of the earth for the lost soul of Queen Pictania. He had the loyalty and aid of his trusted friend, Delano and the stealth and guile of Conrad the hobgoblin.

Trahern became a legendary king of the Bucca and fought alongside King Maccus and his clan against all evil that befouled their lands. They became famous hunters of swamp dragons that terrorised villages and forts across the country.

Vaughan became a well-respected warrior in battles alongside Kael and Breanna. Together they cleared the new lands of evil monsters and foul beasts. Songs were sung about their deeds for years to come. They built a great kingdom in the highlands that they called Pictania. In respect for their mother, they changed the name of their clan and became known as the Picts.

The Picts became a fiercely brave race who never saw defeat. The great Roman Empire, prophesised by Shylah, ravaged Briton for six hundred years, building an empire and crushing the Druids out of existence whilst enslaving the Celts in the southern lands. The descendants of Kael and Breanna were never tamed. The Picts went down in history as fearsome warriors, highly skilled in ambush and rough living. No race of man or beast ever enslaved the Picts and so the Creator's promise was fulfilled.

*

Shylah guarded Excalibur for many years, keeping it safe whilst awaiting the arrival of the boy king who would change the world. Arthur was his name and his fame is still remembered to this day.

The End

About the Author

Robert B Butler was born in Leeds, West Yorkshire, to a family of eight in the early seventies, a great era when the imagination could run wild.

Forming a reading group along with his best friends during his school years captivated his love for fantasy and adventure.

He has a passion for weightlifting, cycling and outdoor adventure. He is a self-confessed keep fit addict and loves nothing better than abseiling off the edge of a clifftop.

His debut book "Celtic Legends- The Search For The White Bear Talisman," draws influences from the classic myths and legends of ancient times. The book has been illustrated by his talented brother, Charles Butler, which adds an extra layer of magic to the work.

Trips around the UK with his family when the children were small heavily influences his debut book and his love of history, folklore and the countryside are all meshed together to create this beautiful story.

A promise to his two daughters to create a story for them to read was the catalyst for this book. Work began way back in 2005 but was left on the back burner due to a career change, only to be picked up again in 2021.

A promise is a promise and at last it's here.

Now that his children are adults and with a grandchild in the picture it might be time to start a sequel.

www.ingramcontent.com/pod-product-compliance
Lightning Source LLC
Chambersburg PA
CBHW020431180626
46812CB00003B/1179